AN IMPOSTOR'S KISS

He was unprepared for the melting smile Meredith bestowed upon him. "Laney," she whispered. "How I adore you. I always knew we would one day be together. I won't fail you. I shall be the perfect wife."

He gave her his best imitation of Laney's smile. And then, as he led her back inside, had the horrid realization that he'd have to marry her in Laney's name if indeed he could not locate his brother by then.

But what troubled Larkin more was the fact he didn't know whether or not he could leave her untouched as she believed Laney would.

He stopped her just before they entered into the light of the lanterns strung near the door. He gazed long and hard at her lovely face, and knew in that instant there was something he must do.

"What is it, Laney?" she whispered when he neither moved or spoke.

He leaned close to her. "This," Larkin murmured, bending his head near to hers. "I must do this."

He kissed her then, covering her sweet mouth with his own and hoping once and for all to get his wanting of her out of his mind.

But he'd been a fool to think such a thing, for the taste of her was that of honey, and the feel of her mouth against his was soft and pliable and far too delicious. And God help them both, but she responded to his kiss like a flower opening to a warm and beguiling sun . . .

ZEBRA'S REGENCY ROMANCES
DAZZLE AND DELIGHT

A BEGUILING INTRIGUE (4441, $3.99)
by Olivia Sumner

Pretty as a picture Justine Riggs cared nothing for propriety. She dressed as a boy, sat on her horse like a jockey, and pondered the stars like a scientist. But when she tried to best the handsome Quenton Fletcher, Marquess of Devon, by proving that she was the better equestrian, he would try to prove Justine's antics were pure folly. The game he had in mind was seduction—never imagining that he might lose his heart in the process!

AN INCONVENIENT ENGAGEMENT (4442, $3.99)
by Joy Reed

Rebecca Wentworth was furious when she saw her betrothed waltzing with another. So she decides to make him jealous by flirting with the handsomest man at the ball, John Collinwood, Earl of Stanford. The "wicked" nobleman knew exactly what the enticing miss was up to—and he was only too happy to play along. But as Rebecca gazed into his magnificent eyes, her errant fiancé was soon utterly forgotten!

SCANDAL'S LADY (4472, $3.99)
by Mary Kingsley

Cassandra was shocked to learn that the new Earl of Lynton was her childhood friend, Nicholas St. John. After years at sea and mixed feelings Nicholas had come home to take the family title. And although Cassandra knew her place as a governess, she could not help the thrill that went through her each time he was near. Nicholas was pleased to find that his old friend Cassandra was his new next door neighbor, but after being near her, he wondered if mere friendship would be enough . . .

HIS LORDSHIP'S REWARD (4473, $3.99)
by Carola Dunn

As the daughter of a seasoned soldier, Fanny Ingram was accustomed to the vagaries of military life and cared not a whit about matters of rank and social standing. So she certainly never foresaw her *tendre* for handsome Viscount Roworth of Kent with whom she was forced to share lodgings, while he carried out his clandestine activities on behalf of the British Army. And though good sense told Roworth to keep his distance, he couldn't stop from taking Fanny in his arms for a kiss that made all hearts equal!

Miss Meredith's Marriage

Lindsay Randall

ZEBRA BOOKS
KENSINGTON PUBLISHING CORP.

ZEBRA BOOKS are published by

Kensington Publishing Corp.
850 Third Avenue
New York, NY 10022

First Printing: August, 1995

Printed in the United States of America

One

It was an uncommonly bleak, July night along the docks of the Thames. Fingers of fog threaded through the twisting, narrow streets as a hired conveyance clattered past ill-kept coffeehouses, lowly taverns, and grimy shops. The two gentlemen seated inside the carriage, however, paid little heed to the inclement weather or the less than illustrious establishments they passed. They were, as usual, deep in discussion and needling each other now and then as good friends, such as they were, often did.

They were both garbed in the finest of English fashion, the only hint of a flaw to their persons being the deep touch of brown to their handsome countenances, compliments of a blazing sun in the West Indies. They were late of Jamaicatown and had just arrived in London a scant half-hour ago.

Only one of the gentlemen, the elder of the two, was actually looking forward to their imminent return to the bosom of the *ton*. The other, younger and yet more jaded than his companion, was most decidedly not looking forward to the event.

"I tell you, Larkin, I intend to write my memoirs once I am settled in Town," said Sir Harry Drake, the elder of the two gentlemen, clearly anticipating once again being ensconced in his flat in St. James Street, "and, b'god, but my collection of notes will prove to be a rousing read!"

The Honorable Larkin Markham pulled a handsome frown. "Gad, Drake, but your poetry is poor enough," he ribbed good-naturedly. "Do not say you intend to suffer the masses with your prose."

Drake, a strapping fellow with dark hair peppered gray, flashed a grin amid his creased but still pleasing face. "That I do! And they'll clamor for more, I tell you, especially when they read the chapters I intend to devote to the adventures you and I have shared."

Larkin's beryl-colored gaze turned quite serious. "I wouldn't mention me, were I you," he advised.

"Never say so! My best tales center around the adventures you and I have shared," insisted Drake. "I'd be a slowtop not to make use of those tales seeing how you have forever been and still remain an enigma to Society, my friend. Like it or not, you intrigued them with your rakehell youth, your stubbornness, and later your capacity to turn your back on the lot of them. You've fanned their collective interest, no doubt about it! And now, the blacksheep of the Graystone legacy is returning to their midst, having amassed a fortune of his own. Ah, but your reappearance in good Society will be the most talked about thing!"

"I'd rather be heading for Jericho," replied Larkin. He parted the curtains of the window near him, staring out into the foggy night, his mood becoming as bleak as the waterfront.

If not for the missive written by his brother, Laney, he would not have returned to England at all. But Laney's note, though brief and rather cryptic, had touched a part of himself Larkin had thought to be long buried. He'd known, even before he refolded the letter, that he must see his brother again, knew too he should mend the tattered threads of his misspent youth. It was time to go home.

Larkin had immediately commenced to end his business in the West Indies. It proved to be a daunting task for he'd amassed numerous holdings and had acquired a staggering fortune during his year-long stay. He'd sent the chosen few possessions he wished to take with him aboard another sailing vessel bound for England and had spent the remaining days seeing to any loose ends. He'd released the servants of his sprawling island home, granting each of them a very comfortable sum of money—more than they'd ever thought to see in their lifetimes—and had dispensed with the notion of hiring a valet for his trip homeward. He'd been dressing himself since the start of his exile, and preferred continuing to do so, at least until he was once again in London. Then, he knew, he must set to the task of making a life for himself.

A life that now, suddenly, would include his brother in some capacity. Odd. He'd thought never to see Laney, or even London, ever again.

Larkin, years ago, had been banished from the Graystone family by his father. His forced exile had not been a common fact; most of the *ton* believed Larkin had simply turned his back on his family due to the fact that he and his father had consistently locked horns over every issue. In particular, Larkin's father had not joined in Larkin's zest in contriving aid for the less fortunate people residing in the countryside of England. While the rich grew richer, the poor folks, most of them destined for a life of near-slavery in the northern factory lands, went without the slightest comfort.

Larkin, an idealist, had thought to buck tradition and lend his aid where he could. But he soon found that without Parliament to back a man, there was naught to be done for the downtrodden of the land. He and his father had engaged in many ugly arguments, while the good son Laney had steered clear of their fiery confrontations.

Then came the most ugliest truth of all; Larkin had overheard his father and mother arguing about him, had witnessed, in fact, his father bring a physical blow to his mother's face. He'd immediately made his presence known, stepping between them and shielding his mother from further harm. His father had become even more livid, his mother dissolving into tears and trying to hide the red welt upon her alabaster cheek. It was at that moment that Larkin felt true hatred for his father. He damned the man, cursed him. His father, incensed, fractured Larkin's nose that night . . . and shattered any illusions Larkin might have had about him.

Within a year, his mother was dead. Larkin blamed his father for her death. In return, he was ousted from the family, cut off from any funds, and left to fend for himself.

Leaving Laney behind was the hardest thing Larkin had ever done.

And now he was returning to London, to Laney. He felt a riot of conflicting emotions surge through him. Why had Laney suddenly written to him? Why now? And why had his brother insisted they meet along the waterfront?

"I wonder if trouble has befallen my brother," Larkin

said, and turned his gaze once again to Drake. "You are certain he was hale when last you spoke with him?"

"Quite," Drake answered. "In fact, he talked of heading to his country estate where he hoped to make some improvements. Sounded to me as though he intended to summer there and perhaps linger until autumn."

"But his letter came from London," Larkin mused. "He should have been clear of the City by then."

"Perhaps he'd had a change of plans," Drake offered.

Larkin shook his head, a wave of rich, coppery hair spilling down over his brow. "My brother, as you know, *never* changes his mind. A decision made for Laney is a decision carried out. He has always been that way. There is nothing done in his life that hasn't been thought out, planned, and planned again."

Drake nodded in agreement. "The two of you always were complete opposites," he said. "Though not in looks. In fact, when I arrived in Jamaicatown to visit you, I was hard-pressed not to think I was staring into Laney's face. You are the mirror image of each other, my friend."

"Looks," said Larkin, "can be deceiving."

"Indeed," Drake murmured. He gave Larkin a measuring glance. "I could never fashion you walking in Laney's boots. He has grown to be a man molded by those around him, you know, while you continue to be dictated by your own passions and fiery temper."

"I guess some things never change."

"Not you, at least," agreed Drake. "You rather like to forge your own way in life. Always have. Laney, however, was never one to cause a stir. He has continued, over the years, to consistently do what he believes is expected of him and nothing less." Drake shook his head in amazement. "Gad, but living such a life must become tiring for one after awhile, don't you think? How your brother remains so perfectly perfect is a puzzle to me . . . especially since *you* have always made a point of being so perfectly *imperfect.* It astounds me that the two of you simultaneously shared the same womb."

"There was never a more mismatched pair than my brother and me," Larkin admitted, "but what a pair we were. . . ."

He gave a small laugh of wonder, thinking of the past, of how things used to be, in the beginning, before life turned ugly. He'd loved his brother—still did, in fact—but he'd never understood him. Larkin felt a stab of regret at having lost contact with his twin so many years ago.

He touched one hand to the pendant he wore looped about his neck. A small sphere of silver, it was meant to symbolize fraternity, trust and love between brothers, and it was the one thing of Larkin's youth, besides the memory of Laney and their too-dear mother, Amabel, that Larkin held dear.

Their mother had gifted them with the pendants on the day they were born. She'd loved them both without abeyance. Indeed, she would have forgiven them anything and stood beside them through the fiercest of storms.

For Larkin, her untamable son whom she most adored, Amabel had done exactly that—and died because of it.

Her death, and the horrid truth behind it, marked the beginning of Larkin's descent into a hell he'd soon come to call home. While the ever-docile Laney continued to do exactly what their overbearing father decreed, Larkin had not. He'd challenged the man, enraged him, and was eventually banished by him, though this last fact was kept within the family circle and harbored there like so many other dark secrets. Larkin had eventually fallen in with a rough lot, haunting the highways and becoming embroiled with the turbulence of starving families in the northern factory lands.

Then came the war, with all its campaigns and loss of life, and for once Larkin found an outlet for his pent-up rage; he became a spy for his country. Just as Laney ascended the Graystone title, Larkin was propelled headlong into a dangerous affair of intrigue and nefarious deeds, all of which further shaped him into the cool, hard-hearted soul he now was.

It had been in Paris that Larkin once again met up with Sir Harry Drake, one of the best spies to ever infiltrate the Continent. Drake had been a close friend of Amabel, and a familiar face at Graystone Manor all through Larkin's and Laney's days in the nursery. It had been Drake who had given Larkin five halcyon days of hunting and riding in the aftermath of Larkin being booted out of school for some prank Larkin could not now remember. Only his mother and Drake had not chastised him.

The second Earl of Graystone, however, had meted out a severe punishment in the form of banning Drake from ever setting foot on Graystone property again, and by blaming and physically abusing Amabel for all of Larkin's shortcomings. It was then Larkin had begun to truly despise his father. Their relationship grew stormier over time, ending in Amabel's death. By that time, Larkin had no idea where his good friend Drake might be and so he'd taken a black path, away from his father and his twin, and into an underworld of highway thieves. Had Drake known of Larkin's troubles, he would have come to his young friend's aid. Alas, they'd not seen each other again until the height of the war. They then became inseparable, watching out for each other and sharing their thoughts.

Larkin and Drake's strong friendship was the only good thing to come of that time on the Continent. They braved thick and thin together. They'd shared losses and victories and narrow escapes, and through it all, Drake had taught Larkin the most difficult lesson of all; he'd taught him how to live with pain, with shattered illusions.

"It is peculiar, don't you think, Harry," Larkin said quietly, using his friend's given name as he often had done during certain times of peril when they'd been alone, weary and wondering if they'd live to see another sunrise, "that my brother should contact me now, after all these years? What do you make of it?"

"A part of me can believe your brother would be the first to bridge the gap between you two. He always hated that you'd gone away."

A lone muscle twitched along Larkin's strong jawline as he remembered the past. "Hell, Drake," Larkin muttered. "I had few choices back then. In fact, I had none."

Drake nodded, knowing all too well how much it had cost Larkin to leave his twin behind.

"And what's the other part, do you think?" asked Larkin.

"The truth? Something smells foul about all of this. I don't know what, though. Laney's letter was too short, too—"

"Cryptic?"

"Exactly."

Larkin agreed. "Laney was never one to dash off just a few short sentences. He loves the written word even more than you, old friend. I can only surmise he is in some sort of trouble or . . . bloody hell, I don't know."

"Mayhap he didn't know quite what to say to you. Perhaps," Drake said gently, "he didn't know how to approach the brother who, in his view, abandoned him those many years ago."

Larkin let out a long, low sigh as he leaned his head back against the squabs. "No doubt that is the whole of it. Damme. How I wish things had been different."

The two gentlemen fell silent for a moment, both lost in their own thoughts.

"Pity the war is over, eh?" Drake finally muttered. "Back then, we knew who and what we were, what was expected of us. Now, however, there remains the matter of resuming our lives . . . whatever the devil that may be. God knows the two of us have spent the last year avoiding that very thing. While you threw your restless energies into creating a fortune in the West Indies, I regrettably spent too much time knocking about, coming and going from Town and searching for that elusive thing called contentment."

Drake gave a slight shake of his head, turning nostalgic. "I hate to say it, Larkin, but I rather liked the intrigue, danger, and what-not of our spying days."

Larkin lifted one brow, a wry smile suddenly appearing on his lips. "As I recall, Drake, it was the 'what-not,' or rather the women, that nearly killed you."

"So it was! But I am like a cat, don't you know? I have nine lives, with only a handful of them spent. I intend to die of ripe old age, and not a moment sooner. God willing, I shall do so on English soil."

Just then, the carriage picked up speed, wheeling through a narrow lane and then turning in a sharp U. Both Larkin and Drake were forced to grab for a hold or be tossed about like sticks.

"Zounds," groused Drake. "Where the devil did this driver learn to handle the reins? I say, Larkin, next time you hire a carriage, take more care in choosing the driver!"

Larkin, planting his rosewood cane with its ivory grip firmly on the floor for leverage, eyed his friend. "I didn't hire this carriage, Drake."

"Nor did I. I thought *you* had."

Both men went perfectly still as the carriage ground to a jarring halt.

"Well, well," muttered Drake, "I wonder what the deuce is going on." He popped open the door, and both he and Larkin, having honed their instincts in far more treacherous territory, both waited before disembarking.

There came no ambush, and it seemed that the driver, somewhat slow and crooked of limb, was intending to climb down off his bench and see them safely outside.

Larkin climbed out, as did Drake who slammed the door and started to step around to speak to the driver.

Suddenly, the hunched man sat up, all signs of crooked limbs gone, slapped the reins to his beast and charged off through the way they'd come. He pulled the horses to a halt at the far end of the alley—the only route of escape for the gentlemen—and then backed the carriage up, securely sealing the lane.

Larkin muttered a curse. "I fear we've been duped, old friend."

"Aye," whispered Drake ominously. "That we have."

The scent of tar and pitch and damp wood was in the air . . . and there was the scent of danger as well. They'd disembarked the carriage at a most inopportune place; in front of them black water sloshed at the docks, on either side of them stood a litter of crates and boxes, and behind them was the alley, now blocked by the carriage. There was nowhere to flee.

A lone lantern lit the crowded space where they stood. The lamp swung once in the wind, and then, with a *ping* of sound and the shattering of glass, the light went out. Someone had thrown a rock at it.

Larkin and Drake were swallowed by darkness and wispy fog. There came the endless slosh of waves interspersed with the sudden, heavy footfalls of intruders.

Larkin held his cane at the ready. "Two of them," he whispered to Drake. "There are two of them coming."

"Aye," answered his friend, though his voice was barely audible. "I hear them. And smell them. Think they're foxed?"

"Possibly."

They shifted, both of them, in the foggy night, their ears, trained by months of spying, centered solely on the ominous footfalls. They gauged the unseen culprits, tallying their strengths, their weaknesses.

"Those nine lives you spoke of earlier, Drake," said Larkin softly, "you might be needing one now."

"I might at that," agreed Drake, chattily enough but clearly centering his thoughts on the coming fight.

They turned back to back, creating a shield for themselves. They both heard the footsteps drawing nearer, heard the two unseen culprits break apart to circle them.

"Reminds me of that time in Paris," whispered Drake, "when that pretty little French thing—Veronique, I think, was her name—led us straight into the lion's mouth. We were outnumbered then, had to fight like the devil, in fact."

"Are you ready to do so again?"

"Just give the word, my friend."

Larkin nodded, waited. He saw a shadowy movement to his left. *"Now."*

They both hurled forward, instinctively knowing where their chosen marks lurked. Larkin was met with a huge piece of wood. He deflected the blow with his left arm while attacking the man's mid-section with his sturdy cane. He wrapped the fingers of his left hand about the wood, yanking it free from the thug's hold, and with a twist of his wrist brought the wood down and in, slamming it against the back of his assailant's knees.

The man howled in dismay, crumbling to the docks, but not before grabbing hold of Larkin's legs. The two of them went crashing to the hard wood of the dock. They wrestled in a horrible struggle, the culprit managing to crash Larkin's skull against the wooden deck with a loud thud.

Larkin, dazed but not defeated, reared up, raising his body, and tossed the man off of him, toppling him over onto his back and straddling him. In a mere moment, Larkin had his cane in both hands and pressed it to the man's windpipe, pinning him.

"Trust me when I say I'd feel little remorse in snuffing the life out of you," he said softly. "Tell me who you are working for."

The man, his bravery knocked out of him, shriveled into a fearful mass of quaking limbs. "I—I know nothin'!" he gasped.

"I doubt that," said Larkin. "Tell me who hired you, and I might just up the ante, pay you in gold, and give you reason to smile the rest of your days."

The man managed a gulp. "You'd do that, mate? Lor', but I never thought you might be better 'n whut the bloke who hired me was."

"His name," said Larkin, applying pressure to the man's throat. "Give it to me. Now."

"If only I could! I—I only know a lady asked me and Bart over there, who is being mauled by yer stout friend, to hire a carriage for you and then meet you on the docks 'ere. She didn't give a name, only said 'er man would be pleased if'n we obliged him. So me and Bart, we came 'ere, waited for yer arrival and then commenced to do what we was paid t' do."

"And that is?"

The man gulped in fear, but clearly decided to tell all or be left for fish feed by the angry and very capable gentleman hovering over him. "Murder," he rasped.

"Whose?" Larkin demanded.

"Yours, o'course."

Larkin glared at him. "And how were you to prove that you'd done the deed? Were you to serve up my head on a platter, perhaps?"

The ugly man would have shook his head had he been able to, but Larkin's cane held him fast to the ground. He licked his dry lips, gasping, "We was told yer silver pendant would be proof e'nuff."

Larkin felt his stomach churn. No one outside of his family had any knowledge of the pendants. How could this brute even know of it?

"This female who contacted you, who is she?"

"I tell you true, I don't know!" the man squeaked. "She—she was only a messenger . . . but a comely one and a lady, I be thinkin'. She wore a cloak and a mask, but I got a peek of 'er 'air, I did. Bright, it was. Like . . . like sunshine.

"That's it? That's all you know?"

The man coughed and struggled for breath as Larkin

applied more pressure with his cane. "I swear, mate, I be tellin' all I know!"

Larkin believed him. Unfortunately, the information he'd gotten wasn't much. In fact, it was all too lacking. He gave the man a stern look. "I'm going to release you now, but if you make one wrong move, I'll see you regret it. Is that clear?"

The man swallowed, winced. "Aye," he whispered. "I won't move, mate. I promise you that."

Larkin eased back, got to his feet. With one hand, he tore at his creaseless neckcloth, yanking it aside and then unfastened the top of his shirt. He shoved one strong hand inside the smooth, snowy material, pulling out his pendant. Yanking hard, he broke the clasp of its chain, letting the silver sphere tumble into his free palm. He tossed the chain down onto the culprit's chest.

"Here is your proof," he said, disgusted. "Take it. Offer it up as evidence that I am truly dead."

The man didn't dare move, but eyed the chain with greed. "And the rest? They no doubt be wantin' t'know what came of the silver sphere you 'ave in yer fist."

Larkin glowered. "Tell them it got lost in the scrape. Tell them whatever you like, but *don't* tell them I still live."

"Me price fer such a thing be high, y'know."

"I don't doubt that," Larkin replied, and his voice dropping a note, added, "and my price for you keeping your end of this bargain will be even higher. If you deceive me, if you so much as whisper a word about what truly happened this night, or if you should even consider blackmail in hopes of more funds, I shall hunt you down. There will be no safe haven for you. I've blunt enough

and the sheer tenacity to dog you until your dying day.
Do you understand what I am saying?"

The man quivered. "Aye. I understand." And then,
whispering, he asked, "But me payment . . . 'ow and
when do I get it?"

Larkin gave him the name and address of his solicitor
on Holywell Street with whom he'd been dealing since
his time in the West Indies, and rattled off an enormous
sum, far more than he probably should have, and most
definitely more than the person who'd hired the thugs
had offered. "I trust this sum is agreeable to you?"

The man had a nasty habit of licking his ugly lips. "It
be enough," he said.

"I thought as much," Larkin replied. He glanced up
and called out for Drake.

"Ho, Larkin!" Drake yelled in answer. "I am here, my
friend, and I've a trophy for my troubles. Victory be-
comes us, does it not?"

"That it does," agreed Larkin, "but let the swine go.
We've no more need of him this night."

"You're certain about that? I say, my friend, I'd like
nothing more than to teach this foul river rat a lesson
he'll not soon be forgetting!"

"Let him go," Larkin repeated.

Drake shrugged, and then did as his friend requested.
Larkin nodded to his own captive, jerking his head once
toward the carriage still waiting at the end of the lane.
"Get out of here. I never want to see your face again."

The man scurried to his feet, massaging his bruised
windpipe with one hand and clutching Larkin's chain
with the other. "Bart!" he gasped, tripping as he scurried
away from Larkin's wrath, "we be rich this night! The

guv has given us a new beginnin'! To the carriage, Bart! Make haste, lest 'e be changin' his mind!"

Larkin and Drake converged on the docks just as the two thugs sped away, heading for the carriage that barred the alley.

"Gadzooks," muttered Drake, gingerly touching a cut above his right eye, "but I fear I'm getting too old for this sort of thing. What the deuce was all that about?"

"Murder," Larkin answered, producing a snowy handkerchief and handing it to his friend.

Drake lifted one brow that was now bright red with blood. "You don't say."

"I do. And if my guess is correct, my brother was sent on a goose chase along the docks this night as well."

Drake, still rather dazed from engaging in fisticuffs with his assailant, let out a slow whistle of disbelief as he dabbed at the cut above his eye. "Leave it to you to be in the eye of every storm, Larkin. Gad, but you haven't even been in London more than an hour, yet here you are, being waylaid by miscreants!"

"Someone hired those thugs for the sole purpose of seeing me dead. It wasn't Laney who penned a letter to me, Drake. I can only surmise that my brother must have received a like missive. If I'm not wrong, I'd say Laney has traveled to these miserable docks as well, hastening to meet someone he expects will be me."

"You don't suppose Laney, on his own, will be met with a similar scenario?"

"That is exactly what I think," answered Larkin.

Drake frowned, knowing Laney would be no match for any cutthroats. "Disaster," he whispered.

Larkin gave a grave nod. "Precisely, my friend. We haven't a moment to lose."

"What do you propose we do?" asked Drake. "Your brother could be anywhere along these docks, or nowhere near them."

Larkin, feeling the pendant he held in his fist burning against his palm, said, "Aye, he could . . . but I've a feeling, old friend, that he is very near. Call it intuition, or even a twin's seventh sense . . . but I'm of the mind that Laney was lured to these docks just as we were. I can't help but believe he isn't far off. No doubt whoever plotted to see me killed alongside the river probably had the same fate in mind for Laney."

Drake muttered an oath. "I shall cut down any lowly being who dares bring harm to him. I'll not rest until I've scoured every inch of these docks in search of Laney, and the whole of London if need be. You have my solemn vow on that, my friend."

Larkin believed him.

Together, he and Drake hurried into the foggy night. They decided to keep to the water's edge in hopes of finding Laney. They didn't have much to go on other than Larkin's hunch that Laney was most likely nearby and had probably been lured to the docks in the same deceitful manner in which he and Drake had been.

Larkin tried not to think of the worst scenario that could occur. He tried not to believe his precious brother might have already met with a foul end, his body tossed into the unheeding current of the river.

But still, horrid images of Laney being cut down haunted him . . . and Larkin had to wonder if he'd be too late to aid the one person still living whom he had ever truly loved.

Two

Lord Lane Markham Graystone gingerly picked his way alongside the darkened docks of the Thames one foggy night in July, and finally admitted to himself that he was not at all the kind of fellow to be gadding about alone in such a dangerous place. He much preferred the comforts of a cozy hearth, a good book, and a glass of sherry to this impenetrable fog and smelly waterfront.

But, alas, he was on a mission this night. He'd come to meet his twin brother, and had been asked to do so alone.

How very like Larkin to insist that they meet under the cover of darkness and in such a lawless part of town, Laney thought. Larkin had forever been a wild and reckless sort. Clearly, he hadn't changed over the years.

Laney suppressed a shiver in the cool, damp air. What a pity he'd been forced to leave behind the safe confines of his hired hackney, but the streets nearest to the docks proved too narrow for the carriage, and so he'd set out on foot.

The earl tried to squash his reservations of being alone along the nefarious waterfront at such an hour, but failed miserably at the task. Laney felt quite overwhelmed by his surroundings; he might as well have been in a foreign country, so out of sorts did he feel.

The awful truth was, he was unutterably lost.

"Blast!" Laney muttered, feeling like a fool. He couldn't just wander around in hopes that he'd stumble upon his brother. What would the ever-dashing, daredevil Larkin think when he found his twin lost, quivering and cowering amid crates of wares and coils of rope? Not much, Laney knew.

He paused beneath a lit lantern, shaking out the creased and now crumpled letter his brother had written to him. It was crumpled because Laney had had to pull it in and out of his pocket too many times to count in the last hour. Every street in this godforsaken part of town looked the same! They were all dirty, each filthy building looking much the same as the next, and if that wasn't depressing enough, the stench of fish and rotting garbage was nigh enough to make a man's toes curl.

Laney suppressed the ungentlemanly urge to use some of his brother's more colorful language choices he remembered from the past. That done, he plucked his quizzing glass from his pocket as well, and then pressed it to his right eye, peering at the words on the paper.

He read the note for perhaps the hundredth time. Yes, yes, he'd taken a left at Willard Lane and then a right and then a left . . . or had he taken a left and *then* a right? Gadzooks, but he could not recall in which direction he'd come!

Pity there was no one about whom he dared query for assistance. There was but a lone vagabond nearby, looking much the worse for wear and smelling quite foul, even from a distance. The miserable-looking soul was hunkered down near a pile of crates, a threadbare blanket draping his hunched shoulders.

Laney frowned, wishing he were safe in his house in

Grosvenor Square, or better yet, back home at his country estate of Graystone Manor, safely tucked away in his library with his books and his ledgers. What he wouldn't give to be *there*.

At the very least, Laney wished he'd been of the mind to bring a companion along with him for this nightly rendezvous. Even his too-uppity manservant, Bigsby, would have proved to be a comfort.

But he'd come alone as Larkin, in his letter, had requested him to do. He'd even opted not to ride in his own carriage, for fear someone would see it along the waterfront and question Laney's presence there. If Larkin wanted to return to London under the cover of darkness, then so be it. For his brother, the third Earl of Graystone would do anything.

Laney had long admired Larkin. He'd hated that his brother had left the family those many years ago—and the fact that their beloved mother, Amabel, had met with a hideous death just a scant week before Larkin's departure had made it all the more difficult to endure. Their mother hadn't even been cold in her grave before Larkin took flight. Their father, the second Earl of Graystone, hadn't so much as batted an eye when he'd learned Larkin had gone, perhaps never to return. Laney decided their father was too deep in grief to notice anything but the absence of his beautiful wife. As for Laney, he'd gone to the privacy of the library, a place where he'd always found comfort, and had fallen to his knees and wept like a baby.

It had taken every ounce of Laney's energy to get through the ensuing months. He'd felt alone and adrift without his mother, and abandoned by his twin. Life, suddenly, had little meaning and felt as though it were filled with cruel Fate.

Years later, when Laney had buried their father and ascended the Graystone title, he'd felt even lonelier. Somehow, the emptiness in him could not be filled. Though losing his parents had been a crushing blow, it seemed to him that one expected one's parents to die first . . . yet one never expected, or could ever be truly prepared, to lose a sibling, especially when that sibling is a twin.

In Laney's mind, it wasn't he who deserved to become the third earl, but Larkin. Larkin was the brave one, the one who, by character alone, deserved the title. Laney had never wished to be the third Earl of Graystone, but he'd ascended his title, and had, in the ensuing years, done what was expected of him.

Laney touched one hand to his breast, finding the silver pendant he wore on a chain about his neck. The pendant proved to be a link with the twin he'd secretly admired all his life. He and Larkin had been like the opposite sides of a coin since the moment of their births, but the pendants they'd been given had been a link of some sort.

There wasn't a day gone by that Laney didn't wear the chain and think of his brother.

He now wondered if Larkin thought of the pendants—or even of him.

Soon, though, they'd see each other once again. Their first meeting might be awkward, naturally, but Laney would right that. He fully intended to embrace Larkin with a tight hug. He'd give him a proper welcome, and hopefully banish all the hurt that must surely lurk in his brother's soul.

Laney hated that no one had ever seemed to understand Larkin. Certainly his brother had been temperamental and headstrong and too often foolish in his youth, but there had been more to the person, Laney knew. There lurked something true and good in Larkin that others never saw, but which Laney forever admired; Larkin, beneath his cool exterior, was a man of deep feeling. Although demanding of those around him, Larkin was even more demanding of his own self. He was, in a sense, his own worst enemy.

Laney only prayed his brother had been happy these many years past.

He tucked away the quizzing glass and the missive and then checked his pocket watch. He was twenty minutes late for the rendezvous. Unfortunately, Laney hadn't a clue where he'd wandered. He could be close to the meeting spot, or could be a league's distance from it.

"Bother," he muttered, vexed with himself for not keeping a clearer head while rounding all those many turns. He'd managed only to confuse himself. He decided he should ask for directions before he missed the meeting entirely.

Gathering his courage and throwing caution to the wind, Laney turned about, fully prepared to ask the doubtless flea-ridden vagabond nearby to point him in the right direction.

As he turned, he saw that the man had shed the filthy blanket and drunk mannerisms. It was then Laney heard the click of a gun's hammer being drawn back.

"Now see here—," Laney began, but realized, too late, the barrel of the gun was trained on him.

There was no time to move, or even think clearly. Laney suddenly heard a *crack,* saw a bluish cloud of smoke, and at the same time felt something hard penetrate his left shoulder.

The impact sent him reeling backwards.

Eyes widening in disbelief, Laney stumbled once, and then crumbled to the dirt and grit beneath him.

Dear God, he thought as he saw a shadow descend. He felt a hand fumble at his throat. His pendant and chain were ripped from his neck . . .

. . . and then he heard footsteps running fast away from him as he lay in a pool of his own blood and misery.

It was morning when he opened his eyes. Or at least he thought it was morning. But no, it wasn't sunlight beating into his brain, but the glow of a lantern. Laney winced, swallowing thickly.

He saw a female face peering down at him. She was pretty, young, and a vision. Her eyes were a warm brown flecked with gold, her hair a beauteous skein of golden strands.

"Am . . . am I in Heaven?" Laney whispered.

"No, sir."

"Then where?" he gasped.

"In a place you ought not have been, obviously," she said, her lovely lips forming a worried frown as she gazed down at him.

"You look like . . . like an angel," Laney whispered.

She shook her head. "I am no angel," she assured him. "My mama, though, she liked to call me her angel, but my father, now *he* claimed I was surely a spawn of the devil."

"No . . . never could you be that."

"And how can you be so certain?"

Laney had no idea. He only knew she was beautiful and precious, and he was glad she was beside him. Her voice was soft, melodious. "You *could* be an angel," he insisted, truly meaning the words. "My angel of mercy," he added. "You see, I—I think I've been shot."

"That you have, sir."

"I am bleeding," he said.

"Buckets," she agreed.

Laney felt panic ripple through his oddly numb body. "If I am to die," he whispered, "I . . . I would rather I did so in your arms. If not that, then with you holding my hand. Would you? H-hold my hand, that is?"

"Here you are bleeding like a pig at the slaughter and you're asking to hold my hand?"

"I am. Amazing, is—is it not?"

"You must be one of those hopeless romantics," she whispered.

"No," he breathed, "though I've wished often enough that I were—or rather, that I could be. You see, I—I am pathetically *un*romantic. Always have been, I fear."

She clicked her tongue. "You make it sound as though such a thing were a dread disease you'd been cursed with."

"I—I've often thought it was. Truth is, I wish I—I could be more romantic . . . one of Byron's corsairs, perhaps, or at least, a—a fellow with more feeling. Alas, I—I am not."

"You seem to be full of feeling now," she observed.

"Maybe the reason is because I am dying." He swallowed heavily. "Lord, I pray I am not soon to meet my end. I'd hate to go to my grave like this."

"Like what, sir?"

"Cold," Laney answered, "and alone."

"But you're not alone. I am here."

He nodded, once, a painful thing to do. "You are at that. And I . . . I am glad."

"You shouldn't talk, sir. You're weak, and bleeding, and you need help."

Laney pressed his eyes shut tight, and saw only visions of his lonely life flash in his mind. "What I am," he said weakly, "is a man who has wasted his youth worrying over right and wrong. I—I don't want to do that anymore. I just want . . ."

"You want what?" she asked, when he faltered.

Laney felt his entire body convulse. He forced his eyes open, staring up at the beautiful woman who'd paused long enough to help a man in trouble.

"I want to cease worrying about what I should or . . . or shouldn't do," he whispered. "I want, simply, to *feel* something. Love someone. I—I want to be ruled by my heart and . . . and not my head."

"I think you just have been," she murmured.

Laney thought, through the fog and his own numbing pain, that there were tears starting to gather in her eyes as she took his hand in hers, holding tight.

"I never met a man who so liked the idea of romance," she said softly.

"Pity," Laney whispered, closing his eyes and relaxing somewhat as their fingers twined together. "Every woman, and man, should know romance." He swallowed heavily, painfully. "You—you feel very nice," he said. "Warm. Friendly."

She gave a soft, self-deprecating laugh. "Yes, I am that. Friendly. That's me."

Laney forced his eyes open. "Your name. What is it? May I ask?"

"Imagine, a dying man being so polite. Of course you can ask. My mama named me Wren; claimed I was tiny, like a bird."

"Wren. What a pretty name. What are you doing here, Wren?"

"Wasting precious time, no doubt. You need help, sir."

"I do," Laney agreed. "But I—I am afraid it might be too late."

"No," she whispered, suddenly leaning her mouth close to his ear. "Don't you say or even think such a thing, do you hear? It isn't too late. It's never too late for a gentleman as polite and sweet as you seem to be."

Laney smiled, though it hurt him to do so. "I—I came here to find my brother, did I mention that?"

She must have shaken her head in answer, but Laney felt only the curls of her hair brushing softly against his face. Nothing, in all his life, had ever felt so pleasant as her silky, fragrant hair whispering against him.

Laney swallowed convulsively, trying to keep his head clear. "I'm to meet my brother here, or—or somewhere nearby. Lord, but he'll think I—I'm a sorry excuse for a man if he finds me in such a state. He'll be . . . most upset."

"He might," agreed Wren, worrying over him. "What do you say we get you cleaned up and right as rain before you meet your brother?"

He attempted to tip a grin up at her. "I'd say that would be a neat trick, considering my precarious position." His words, Laney realized, were beginning to slur together.

Wren frowned. "Do you think you can walk?"

"I shall try," he said, making a motion to sit up. But

he merely managed to lift his head an inch or two and then felt it plop back down with a thud.

"Lie still," Wren insisted. "I'll get help."

Laney felt her move away from him with a rustle of her skirts. "Don't . . . don't leave. Please."

Of a sudden, she bent down, smoothed a strand of coppery hair from his brow, and whispered, "I'll return, sir. That's a promise."

She said the words with such sincerity that he could do no less than believe her. "I—I'll wait then," he murmured, his eyelids feeling as though they were weighted with lead.

"Do that, sir," she whispered. And then she was gone.

Laney let his eyes drift shut as he breathed deep of the lingering scent she left behind.

She smelled like violets blooming in a rich field.

She smelled like life.

He prayed she would return. Such was his last thought before his world went totally black.

Three

On a late summer day, Miss Meredith Sophia Darlington, late of a nuncheon with her friends of the Midnight Society, and accompanied by her flighty maid, Betsy, as well as her dearest friend, the elderly Lady Peach Beveridge, arrived along the busy Magazine of Hyde Park. She and her companions were comfortably ensconced in Meredith's fashionable barouche and four, and were being driven about by her seasoned and trustworthy coachman, Boyle.

The healthy breeze of a cool, nearly autumn day caught at Meredith's stylish bonnet, sending the loose ribbons trailing over one slender shoulder as her amber-colored eyes studied the vehicles teeming near her. It seemed all the city was awheel on this bright and breezy day. Those of good Society who'd recently returned to Town from their summer excursions had come to see and be seen.

As for Meredith, she'd come to find a bridegroom.

"The second vehicle to yer left, Miss Meredith. That be the one," offered the coachman over one shoulder.

"Thank you, Boyle," said Meredith. She could always count on her coachman's sharp eye—and his discreet sensibilities.

Meredith leaned nervously back against the squabs and

watched from the corners of her eyes as the aforementioned high-perched phaeton approached. It was the perfection of neatness, with a yellow body made sleek-looking with black lines and an undercarriage coated in black as well. Two beautiful bays, obviously bred for speed and matched by a skillful eye, led the smart conveyance. A handsome driver, clearly a master at keeping his spirited team in hand, rode on the bench.

Meredith would recognize the man's face anywhere—what she could see of it, anyway, without her blasted spectacles. Indeed, her heart lurched at the somewhat blurred sight of the third Earl of Graystone. Blurry or not, the man cut a handsome figure. Had it actually been almost seven years since she'd last laid eyes on Lane Markham Graystone? Amazing. It felt like yesterday.

The carriages met neck and neck just as a brisk wind claimed Meredith's hastily tied bonnet. The bonnet, with its flouncy pink gauze, skittered over the folded top of the barouche, whirled in the air for the briefest moment, then twirled down toward the hard surface of the road.

A quick, gloved hand caught the bonnet in midair. The fawn-covered hand belonged to none other than the Earl of Graystone. He tipped his beaver her way.

"I shall return your bonnet to you," he promised gallantly, just as his stylish carriage whisked by.

Meredith tried to hide her dismay—and her pleasure. Gracious, but she hadn't meant to capture the earl's attention in such a public way.

"Forget taking another roundabout, Boyle. Head for home," Meredith ordered, suddenly uncertain of what she planned to do this day. There'd be no chance for a clandestine meeting betwixt herself and the enigmatic earl. In truth, coming to the Park in hopes of speaking with

Lord Graystone had been a very foolish idea; there was a crush of carriages and people about, as there always was at such an hour.

Boyle turned on his seat to give her a dubious frown. "Sorry I am, ma'am, but the Fleming daughters, what with their landau, huge postillion, and their pair of long-tailed Arabians, have blocked the lane. We've no choice but to make the round again, lest o' course we sit and wait for them to get a move on."

Meredith gave the order for Boyle to move on. She had no mind to wait while the spoiled Fleming girls, Ethelinda and Eunice, made up their minds as to whether they'd brave the course round the Park yet again, or take the road back to the heart of Town.

Boyle clicked his team to life just as the Fleming landau lurched forward and the lively Arabians plunged back into the line of carriages. Boyle and his team were forced to wait yet again while the Fleming carriage rudely forced its way into line.

Meredith did her best to contain her agitated nerves. She'd come to Hyde Park only to seek out the handsome and enigmatic Lord Graystone. Certainly her plan had been outlandish at best, and demeaning at the least. But Meredith was in a fix.

She must, by the time she turned three-and-twenty, be ensconced in the home of her chosen bridegroom. Her father, Manningford, always a stickler for details in life, and even in death, it seemed, had left nothing to chance concerning his vast worldly possessions, as well as his extremely independent-minded daughter. Should Meredith not find any gentleman to her liking before the appointed date, Manningford had left an iron-clad will giving Meredith's godmama, the duecedly outrageous Phoebe, sister to the unorthodox Penelope Barrington—who was godmama to Meredith's cousins—full power to choose Meredith's intended.

Though Meredith adored her godmama, whom she lovingly called Aunt Phoebe, she did not fancy allowing the outlandish woman such free rein with her future. Indeed, Aunt Phoebe might very well see fit in betrothing Meredith to one of the Arab princes who often graced Penelope Barrington's country estate, Stormhaven, in the Cotswolds as it was no secret that the wild sisters loved to entertain at Stormhaven. Or perhaps the eccentric Aunt Phoebe would choose one of the many Americans with whom she had shared adventures, or even, one of the secret agents who had slipped mysteriously between France and England during the height of Napolean's campaigns via Aunt Phoebe's network of estates cast across Europe like dice.

No, Meredith had no mind whatsoever of allowing Aunt Phoebe to choose her groom. And since Meredith's fateful natal day was just a fortnight away—and seeing as how Meredith had yet to find any gentlemen who'd offered for her to her liking—she'd decided to take matters into her own hands; she would choose her own bridegroom.

She had chosen Lord Lane Markham Graystone.

"Truly, Merry," said Meredith's reasonable and very intuitive elderly friend, Lady Peach Beveridge, sitting beside her. "I do not think you should chase his lordship in such an open manner. Far better it would be to slip him a note and have him meet you at some out of the way place, say, in Lady Anderby's maze of a garden during her costume ball set for Thursday next."

"Need I remind you my natal day is but a fortnight

away? Thursday next will be too late," said Meredith. In afterthought, she added, "And I am hardly 'chasing' the man, Peach."

"But you did manage to have your bonnet whisked away at the precise moment. Very clever of you, my dear."

"Clever? Hardly," Meredith assured her friend. "Peach, you of all people know I've a nasty habit of losing things. All we Darlington women do."

"If you're referring to the spectacles you believe you've lost, they are in your reticule, my dear. I saw you place them there earlier."

"My reticule? Ah, so they are. I had feared I'd dropped them while climbing into the carriage." Meredith, hating her spectacles perhaps as much as she hated the idea of marriage, ignored them and then gave her friend a warm smile. "Whatever would I do without you, Peach?"

"Marvelous things, no doubt. You're far too harsh on yourself, darling. And why you think you must cast yourself upon the nails of matrimony only to appease that ridiculous will of your father's is beyond me."

Meredith frowned. "Either I choose my intended, or my godmama will choose the man for me. You and I both know Aunt Phoebe—just as her wild sister, Penelope—has never been prudent when it comes to matters of the male gender. Why, between the two of them, they've married and buried more husbands than I dare to count! And," she added, her voice lowering, "I shan't wish to mention how many lovers they've known. The godmamas of we Darlington women are notorious for finding interest in the most shocking of men. You know what I say is true. And so, I shudder to think what type of male Aunt Phoebe would deem appropriate for me!"

"Still," insisted Peach, "I do have to wonder why you've chosen Graystone. I wouldn't be a friend if I didn't caution you, Meredith. The man is quite changed of late. Everyone says so—and you, too, would have had heard the rumors if you hadn't been off visiting your cousin Marcie in the wilds of Cornwall." She mocked a shudder. "Really, Merry, what you found of interest in that windy, pedestrian place is beyond me!"

"I found my cousin," Meredith softly reminded her friend. "And her husband as well. In truth, I had a lovely visit."

"One that lasted nearly a year! Heavens, Merry, but you have been away from good Society for too long. You've become too far removed from what is happening here."

"Peach, you know I've never been one to care overly much about parties and soirees . . . and besides," Meredith added, "I am not of blue blood, so what difference did it make, really, that I chose to linger with Marcie and her dashing marquis as they revisited the place of Marcie's youth?"

"The difference, my dear, is that you missed the entire last Season, and a chance to find a husband, to boot."

"But I've only *now* decided to marry," Meredith gently reminded Peach.

"My point exactly." Lady Beveridge sighed dramatically. "How like you to go willy-nilly off to the wilds when you should have gone a-hunting for a suitor. Dear Merry, you shouldn't leave everything until the last moment. What is it about you Darlington cousins that makes you so hungry for adventure that you give not a whit of thought to the truly pressing matters of life?"

"Like finding a husband?" Meredith asked, knowing exactly that was what Peach meant.

"Yes, finding a husband." Her friend harrumphed. "Now, mind you," she added, softening, "I wouldn't be scolding you so but for the plain truth you obviously feel indebted to carrying out your father's dying wish. I know how much you and your cousins adored your doting fathers, and that all of you have contrived to do exactly what those magnificent men decreed—"

"But," Meredith interrupted, smiling, "there *is* a 'but' coming in this speech of yours, is there not?"

"But of course there is," Peach replied, "otherwise I'd have never opened my mouth! The plain fact is, Merry, I don't think your wonderful father would have insisted you marry at all if he'd lived to see what a gem you've become and how wonderfully you've managed to handle what small part of your vast inheritance you've been able to control. In fact, Manny would have been most pleased, I'm certain. Which brings me to my next point . . . you should *not* set your sights on Lord Graystone."

"Because he is 'changed?' "

"That and a great deal more," insisted Peach. "He isn't at all the man for you, Merry, mark my words. Why, until a month ago, he would have been perfectly content to barricade himself inside his extensive library at Graystone Manor."

"What is so terrible about that?" murmured Meredith, for she, too, often preferred a good book to a room full of company.

"Not a thing, of course, if the man had shown any interest in the female sex—which he never really had. But here now, that isn't the point of my telling you about Graystone."

"Pray tell, what *is* the point then?" Meredith asked, her patience beginning to ebb.

Peach leaned closer. "The man, of late, is most unlike himself, I dareswear. There are shades to him now that hadn't been there before. I can't say precisely what it is, Merry, but I know for certain there is an edge to his character that wasn't present a few months ago. He seems more aloof, cooler and well, *dangerous*."

"Oooh, yes," chimed in Meredith's maid, Betsy, who was seated across from Peach and Meredith. "He is a bit dangerous now! I be thinking the reason is because his twin brother, the badseed Larkin, is rumored to have been set upon by river thieves, murdered and then tossed into the water! Can you imagine such a thing?" Betsy gave a dramatic shiver. "I'd be acting a bit mysterious myself if I thought someone had murdered my kin and was thinking to do the same to me. But truly, Miss Merry," she added with heartfelt sincerity, "I hear the ladies aren't so adverse to the change in his lordship. I be thinking they rather enjoy him acting so mysterious-like. And the gentlemen, I hear tell, are quicker to make way for him now. Why, he has everyone abuzz, he does!"

Meredith lifted her brows, eyeing her maid in a new light. She hadn't realized the gossipy Betsy, who'd been away from the city, traveling with Meredith, knew so much about Graystone . . . but then again, the servants in every household often knew as much, if not more, than their employers.

"What your maid says is true enough," Peach added hastily. She gave Meredith a serious look. "Though a good many Beauties would gladly marry Graystone in an instant—and have certainly let him know this—any level-headed female would know enough to now stay away from him. His lordship hasn't been the same since rumors of his brother's unfortunate demise began spreading around the city. He blows hot and cold, and there are moments when his temper is so volatile that one would think they were dealing with his ne'er-do-well twin, Larkin. As for what truly happened to his rakish brother, the earl has been extremely tight-lipped, neither acknowledging or disavowing the rumor that his brother was accosted near the docks and thrown into a watery grave. In fact, he has been evasive and in a decidedly foul mood. Now I ask you, Merry, is that the type of man with whom you'd like to spend the rest of your life? One whose temper can flare at a moment's notice?"

Meredith sat back, digesting all she'd heard.

So Laney had changed, had he? Well, she'd expected as much.

In spite of all she'd heard, Meredith still held steady to the course of choosing Laney as her intended. The simple fact was that Meredith and Laney had at one time shared a special bond. She'd helped save him from a nasty encounter during a summer holiday she'd spent at Graystone Manor with her father, and Laney in turn had sweetly promised to one day return her favor.

Meredith still believed in Graystone's sense of honor and his inherent goodness, all rumours of his now-mercurial temperament aside. But most important of all was the fact that Laney had shared with Meredith a deep secret about himself . . . a secret which Meredith knew made him the perfect choice as her intended, and she for him.

"I appreciate what you've told me this day," said Meredith, "but I have made my decision and I intend to see it through to the end."

"Oooh!" gasped Betsy, all at once intrigued, delighted and a bit nervous about her mistress's choice.

Peach, knowing she could never gainsay her young friend when Meredith set her mind to something, sighed.

"Very well, my dear, if you are intent on wooing Lord Graystone, I shall do what I can to help, but do know I cannot understand why you've chosen him above all the many admirers you have," Peach said.

Meredith knew exactly why she had chosen the earl. He'd captured a tiny part of her heart when she'd been but ten-and-six, and since that brief time they'd shared, she had never forgotten his gentleness, his thoughtfulness, and most especially his *secret*.

The barouche came to a grinding halt. Meredith tried to see beyond Boyle's massive bulk seated atop the high bench before her.

"Is there trouble?" she asked.

"That blasted landau again, ma'am. They've broken a wheel, they have. Their liveried coachman is naught but a greenhorn. Still wet behind the ear, he is. Can barely keep his team in hand, let alone manage the upkeep on that fine carriage."

Meredith had no choice but to give Boyle the word to go to the aid of the younger coachman. Boyle, like all great coachmen, took huge pride in his skill and abilities. Before she knew what he was about, a preening Boyle took charge of the chaos and created some semblance of order as he helped direct the traffic and oversaw the difficult task of clearing the way for the other vehicles.

"Well, I daresay we shall be in for a long wait," announced Peach, peering through her lorgnette at the busy scene.

"Indeed, we shall," agreed Meredith.

She could have easily ordered Boyle to move around the phaeton, knowing there were many others near to lend assistance, and thus afford herself the luxury of leaving the crowded lane. But seeing Boyle puff with pride and throw himself wholeheartedly into the task at hand pleased Meredith.

Meredith had always made it a point to know her servants; she knew of their dreams and their problems. Having lost her beloved parents and having no siblings, Meredith's servants were more like family to her than anything else. She would not spoil Boyle's moment of taking charge of the situation.

Her abigail, Betsy, having craned her neck to view the scene, let out a breath of delight, then plopped herself back down on the cushion. "Coo, Miss Meredith, but I do believe your handsome earl is headed this way!"

Meredith felt her heart race as she espied Graystone's spanking phaeton drawing near.

Betsy shivered with heady anticipation. "Quick," she whispered. "Have you nothing else to let fly with the wind?"

"Certainly not," Meredith replied.

Betsy wasn't listening. "Mayhap you could use my kerchief. It is a bit wrinkled and all, but it smells of that fine lavender scent you like so much. I do confess that I spilt just a tad out of the bottle this morn, but don't be worried. I mopped it up quick, I did."

Betsy pressed a square of squashed linen into Meredith's gloved hand, grinning from ear to ear.

Peach rolled her eyes heavenward. "One of these days, dear Merry, your servants, who are just as spirited as you, will go too far!"

Chastened, the abigail lowered her eyes. "I only

knocked two bottles of scent off the dressing table, truly I did. And I made certain to get the stain out of your carpet . . . least I think I did."

Meredith gave her maid a pat on the knee. "Do not fret so, Betsy. I am not angry." She returned the girl's handkerchief. "Nor am I of the mind to allow any more of our possessions to 'fly with the wind,' as you put it."

Betsy's brown curls bobbed as she lifted her face to her mistress's. "Oh, but however will you capture his lordship's interest again if'n you don't lose something he can fetch?"

Is that what Betsy thought she'd done, purposely lost her bonnet at the precise moment the earl's carriage passed by? If so, then what must his lordship have deduced?

No doubt the same.

Meredith felt her face flush as Lord Lane Markham Graystone expertly handled his team, leading them through a U shape and halting neatly behind her barouche.

Meredith didn't need eyes in the back of her head to know that the handsome earl had secured his ribbons with his groom and had dropped down off his bench.

There came the sound of sure footfalls on the lane.

"La," Betsy breathed. "He has eyes only for you, Miss Merry!"

"Hush," Meredith whispered. She knew Laney well enough to know he'd not be dreamy-eyed over any female. But still, she couldn't stop the excitement that whirled through her. Her chance of speaking with Laney again was nearly upon her.

Betsy threw a wide-eyed look past Meredith. "Coo, but he is a fine gentleman. And look! He's carrying your bonnet, Miss Merry. Carrying it as though it were a crown of gold, he is!"

Meredith wrinkled her nose at Betsy's romantic drama. Such fustian. Meredith should have had the good sense to leave Betsy at home this day, but the girl had thrown Meredith one of her soulful, doe-eyed glances when Meredith had announced to the staff she'd be spending the day at her Ladies' Club. Betsy, forever pining that she wished to "prop up her toes" in Lady Anderby's fine kitchen in Hanover Square, had made such a cake of herself that Meredith, hoping to brighten the girl's day, had asked her abigail to come along as chaperon.

Meredith now rued such a decision.

"He's drawing nearer, Miss Merry," whispered Betsy. "Lordy, I fear I'm going to faint!"

Peach muttered something about ill-bred servants.

Meredith gave her abigail a cautionary look. "Enough, Betsy, do you hear?"

"Yes, miss," said Betsy, dropping her lashes just as Lord Lane Markham Graystone stepped beside the carriage.

"Ladies," said his lordship in greeting. He sketched a bow, tipping his hat.

Meredith, finally face to face with the man she'd set her sights to marry, found herself absurdly tongue-tied. She hadn't guessed that seeing him again would affect her so profoundly, hadn't realized, until this moment, how very much she'd been looking forward to seeing him again. Never in her adult life had she felt the odd tremor of nervousness as she did now staring at the fine face of Lord Graystone. No doubt the reason was due to the fact she'd come to the Park hoping to see him and intending to strike a bold bargain with him.

Peach took that moment to speak. "Lord Graystone, what a gallant saviour you are," she said. She tucked away her false-needed lorgnette, eyeing Graystone with a hawk's clear sight. "It seems Miss Darlington's coachman has been pressed into service by the unlucky driver of yonder landau, and here we sit in this blinding heat."

Blinding heat? thought Meredith. The day was unseasonably cool.

"Pray, allow me to make introductions," continued Peach. "Lord Graystone, this is my dearest, dearest friend Miss Meredith Darlington."

Meredith smiled. "Truly, Peach, there is no need for such a formal introduction," she said, receiving a surprised look from her friend. "Lord Graystone and I are old acquaintances, are we not, my lord?"

Graystone, hearing Meredith's words, gave her his complete attention. His eyes held hers, and Meredith had the distinct impression he was measuring her.

For one horrible moment Meredith wondered if she'd erred in believing he would remember her for there was no spark of familiarity in his green gaze, and the way in which he finally reached for her hand was one of practiced politeness, nothing more.

Meredith felt her heart fall.

Perhaps he noticed some telltale reaction in her to his less than exuberant greeting for in the next moment, his eyes warmed and his smile deepened. "My pleasure to see you again, Miss Darlington," he said. He placed a light kiss to her gloved fingers, his gaze not wavering from her own.

Meredith had to suppress a surprising tingle of warmth spreading up her spine as his lips seemed to burn through the soft kid of her glove. How very unlike her to actually *tingle* in a man's presence! And the fact that it was Laney who made her feel such a sensation was most peculiar indeed. They'd been friends for one brief summer Holiday, had shared secrets and dreams . . . but she'd never once been so *affected* by him as she seemed to be now.

Meredith couldn't help but notice how Laney had outgrown the rangy figure she remembered. Now trim and muscled, he was indeed a handsome swell. He cut a dashing figure in his exquisite, finely tailored blue coat, buff breeches, and highly polished Hessians. His hair, beneath his tall beaver, was the shade of burnished copper, his eyes the color of beryl fire.

How odd, thought Meredith, transfixed by the sight of him, but she couldn't for the life of her remember Laney's eyes being quite so startling in color, nor his hair such a bold coppery shade. In truth, she couldn't recall Laney ever being so much larger than life as he seemed to her now. Memory—and the passage of time—must have dulled his image, she thought. Yes, that must be it, she decided; she'd quite forgotten how very handsome Lord Lane Markham Graystone could be.

His lordship released her hand, and then lifted his other hand in which he held her lost bonnet.

"I believe this belongs to you, Miss Darlington." He passed the still perfectly shaped bonnet with its pink gauze up to her.

Meredith took the bonnet, murmuring her thanks, and then placed it atop her head, glad for the task at hand and that she could center her thoughts on something other than the fact that Laney was now standing before her in the flesh.

The moment was nothing as she'd envisioned. She had hoped he would be more enthusiastic at the sight of her.

But then again, the Laney she remembered had been quiet and introspective. Of course he would not gush over seeing her again!

Meredith smiled warmly, hoping to let him know with the gesture that she remained the close confidant he'd known nearly seven years prior.

Graystone acknowledged the private smile, bestowing one of his own upon her . . . but the features she remembered as being soft and unalarming, were now strong-boned and startling in their handsomeness. And his intense green eyes were disturbing at such close proximity. If she hadn't known better, she'd have deduced that he'd grown up to be a man who had broken his share of female hearts.

Graystone nodded to the commotion in front of them. "It seems," he said, "that we are all stranded here for the time being. I doubt the lane will be cleared for another thirty minutes or so."

Peach, having kept quiet long enough, spoke up. "My thoughts exactly," she agreed, still eyeing Meredith with a quizzing look. She obviously was intrigued that Meredith hadn't told her she and Lord Graystone were already acquainted, and the fact that they *were* acquainted was an advantage Peach just as obviously was not going to allow to be wasted. "What a pity, too, for Miss Darlington had hoped to enjoy the park this afternoon, hadn't you, dear friend?"

Meredith instantly sensed to what conclusion Peach was leading the conversation—just as she sensed that she'd surprised Laney with reminding him they'd previously met.

"I do not mind the wait," said Meredith, suddenly rethinking her choice of seeking out Graystone in such a public place. Far better it would have been to meet with him in private. Laney, after all, had always been a very private person.

"Of course you do," insisted Peach. "You said yourself you wished to take in some air and stretch your legs. Lord Graystone, surely you would not object to a stroll with the lovely Miss Darlington?"

Graystone's beryl-colored eyes held on Meredith's for a tad longer than necessary before he looked to Peach. In that brief span of time, Meredith saw a flash of what could only be discerned as intrigue. Yet, there was something more that shimmered in his gaze. It took her a moment to realize what that *something* was: wariness mixed with suspicion.

Meredith quelled a frown. Could her dear, sweet Laney perhaps think she'd grown to be very much like the out and outers who pined for his attentions and would go to any lengths to obtain it—even something so silly as losing their bonnet for him to retrieve? She hoped not, just as she hoped she'd have a chance to prove to him that she wasn't at all devious.

"A walk in the park?" he replied, clearly tumbling the idea over in his mind. After a moment of consideration, he surprised her by saying, "Excellent idea. May I be so bold as to offer my arm to you fine ladies?"

"Surely, you may," said Peach, pleased, "but I must decline. My rheumatism, you know. It's been acting up of late. I'm not as quick as I once was. But I'll not think to discourage you and Miss Darlington and, of course, her abigail from taking a quick stroll down the nearest path. Pray, enjoy yourselves and know that I am most comfortable sitting here and watching all the commotion."

Graystone nodded. "If you are certain."

"I am," insisted Peach.

"And Miss Darlington?" he asked. "What say you?"

What indeed? thought Meredith, her heart sinking when he did not address her simply as his "merry Meredith," as he'd been wont to do that summer long ago. But for Meredith to decline would be most unseemly. Too, she firmly reminded herself, she'd come to Hyde Park to strike a bargain with Laney. She shouldn't stray from her plan now. As for Laney's somewhat blunted affect, surely it was because he was now an earl; he couldn't go about with his emotions unchecked.

Meredith accepted, moving to take Graystone's proffered arm. She felt her heart trip as she touched her hand to his sleeve. He was indeed solidly built, no doubt having toned his muscles with the reins of his thoroughbred team.

Though she'd come with a proposal of a platonic marriage in mind, now that he was so near, Meredith wondered whether or not she would dare see her plan through to fruition—and even, if she should.

The Laney of her youth had *never* set her heart aflutter as he was doing now. And she knew, without a doubt, that Laney wouldn't be pleased if he knew of her physical reaction to him.

Heavens, thought Meredith, as Graystone helped her out of the coach, but the day wasn't going at all as planned! In fact, it was progressing in quite the opposite direction, and was far worse than she'd ever imagined.

The simple fact was, though Meredith had marriage in mind, she hadn't at all considered the possibility she might actually be *attracted* to the man Lord Lane Markham Graystone had become.

Four

"How fortunate that his lordship caught your bonnet, don't you think, Miss Merry?" whispered a too-eager Betsy, walking behind Meredith. "I knew something exciting would happen today! And do you know why? Because I spilled not only your perfume, but some salt as well, and me mum always did say that salt spilled meant a prodigious happening about to take place. Did you ever hear that sort of thing, Miss Merry? Salt and happenings?"

"No, Betsy. I hadn't," Meredith quietly replied, and then shot her abigail a warning glance.

Betsy took the cue, falling silent.

It was too late; Graystone had heard Besty's remark.

He leaned his head towards Meredith's, whispering, "Think you that our stroll is a 'prodigious happening,' Miss Darlington?"

His movement brought the clean, manly scent of him to settle around Meredith. The effect his essence had on her was both jarring and thrilling, and not at all what she'd expected to feel when once again in his presence.

Meredith strove to find her voice. "I'd call it unexpected, my lord," she replied.

"Would you?" There was a challenging light in his green eyes.

Meredith felt herself bristle. "I had nothing to do with the Fleming daughters losing a carriage wheel," she pointed out.

"And your bonnet?" he asked boldly.

So he did think—as Betsy and Peach believed—that she'd intentionally lost her bonnet! Meredith felt herself blush pink.

"Really, Laney," she replied, unable to help herself and falling into the use of his given name and her age-old habit of wearing her emotions on her sleeve, "you should know me better than that. It was whisked away by the wind, nothing more."

He seemed, however briefly, amazed she would address him by his given name. And then, just as quickly, the surprise dissipated. He gave her what appeared to be an easy, wide grin. "A most fortuitous wind for me then," he replied.

How smoothly he'd turned his words into a compliment! Meredith wondered again at the stark change in Lord Graystone. Peach had warned her about the transformation in Laney, and certainly people changed over time, but the man strolling beside her and the Laney she remembered, had *always* remembered, were so profoundly at odds that Meredith wondered if the Laney of her past had ever existed at all.

They headed for a copse of trees, crossing over lush lawns and beneath tree branches all abloom with the green leaves of late summer. The air was fragrant, and sunshine dappled the tended grounds as birds twittered and flew from branch to branch. The cool day might have been perfect had not Meredith been thinking of marriage between herself and the man walking beside her.

Was it her imagination, or had he truly not recognized

her? Albeit, Meredith had been a gawky miss of sixteen, and he a titled heir of one-and-twenty who had been about to embark on an extended tour, his mind no doubt centered solely on his impending travels . . . but still, there surely must exist some sense of recollection in his brain, thought Meredith.

Never would she forget the way in which Laney had taken her hand in his and kissed her palm with such sweetness on the morning she'd saved him from certain scandal. And never would she be able to forget the sincerity in his words when he'd said he would return her favor should she ever find need of him. For all time, he had fervently promised, he would remember her.

So much for Laney's memory, she decided, agitation suddenly brewing in her breast. Caught up in her own brown thoughts, Meredith missed the first part of Graystone's sentence.

". . . seems to have lost a shoe," he finished.

Meredith blinked. "Beg pardon?"

"Your abigail," he explained. "She seems to have somehow lost her shoe."

Meredith turned to find her maid hopping on one foot.

"Fancy that!" cried Betsy. "My shoe came clean off, it did. Now I've gone and ruined my stocking in the grass. Don't you worry, though, Miss Merry. Continue your walk. I'll just be a minute fetching my shoe and cleaning my stocking, I will. I'll catch up, I promise."

Meredith knew exactly what her spirited maid was up to. "We shall wait for you," she said.

Betsy waved the very notion aside. "Oh, I wouldn't dream of it, miss!" The girl made an utter widgeon of herself as she limped back the way they'd come, in search of the mysteriously missing shoe.

"It would seem," said Graystone, "that your maid is bent on having time to herself this day." *Or seeing that the two of us have time alone,* his look seemed to convey.

Meredith felt her face pale. The earl was not at all a slowtop, nor was he the Laney she remembered. Why, oh why, had she undertaken this ridiculous idea of seeking him out?

"There is a bench beneath a shade tree not far from here where we can wait on your abigail," he said, once again cutting into her thoughts. "Shall we press on?"

Meredith could only nod. She'd begun something she couldn't stop. Not now. Not when she'd come this far. Finally, she would have a moment alone with Laney. And though this man she'd known only briefly in the past had proved to be nothing at all as she remembered, she still held onto the notion that perhaps he wasn't so changed and would help her with her predicament.

To her abigail, she called, "Do join us once you find your shoe."

Betsy smiled, waved, and continued to hop along the path, clearly intending to prolong her search.

Graystone led Meredith on toward the promised bench.

The world, for Meredith, seemed suddenly to close around them. The call of the birds, the rustle of the breeze, even the sounds of a few carriages squeezing past the congestion on the lane behind them sounded muffled and a lifetime away.

There was just the two of them.

Alone.

And though Meredith tried not to, she felt sixteen again . . . and vulnerable, far, far too vulnerable.

* * *

Beautiful, that's what she was, he thought as they walked side by side beneath an archway of tree boughs.

It had been her eyes that first captured his interest when she'd lost her bonnet and he'd played the gallant and had reached out to pluck it from midair before it tumbled to the hazard of dust, carriage wheels and horses' hooves of the lane below. Her eyes were not a simple blue, or brown or gray, but amber; amber with fire in them.

Her hair was a lustrous gold, full of ringlets and a few stray strands that curled beguilingly about her finely boned features. Hers was the face for a locket, surely, or a painting by one of the great masters.

Or perhaps, even, a face that could cause men to duel at dawn, or to gamble away their fortunes, their hearts, even their souls.

She had a mouth made for kissing; pouty and full and ever mobile. Her skin was pure and unblemished. And her body, so perfectly sheathed in a blush-pink gown with an unbuttoned gray silk spencer . . . ah, now *that* was a sweet treasure all it's own.

But there was yet another caveat to her, he sensed: she was, obviously, the woman he'd been hoping to meet.

This last thought caused his jaw to tighten. He must remember not to become enchanted by her lest he make a dangerous mistake. To falter now would be to put his own life at risk, and that of a beloved other. To become too enthralled by this female, no matter how pretty or desirable she might prove to be, would mean the downfall of all his plans.

It was a danger he would not forget.

Meredith chanced a peek at Laney, not missing the glance he'd sent in her direction. He walked with his back perfectly straight, his head held high. His stride was easy, relaxed, but in it could be discerned the centuries of wealth and good breeding that had been his on the day of his birth. That he was a titled gentleman, a great personage with a family name that spanned far back into the exalted past of England, could not have been mistaken by anyone, least of all Meredith.

But beneath the polish, the distinguished walk, and even the fine handsomeness of the man, there simmered, Meredith guessed, a temper not to be matched. She noted how his jaw tightened a moment ago when he'd glanced at her. The sight of it troubled her.

She realized, perhaps a shade too late, that her resolve to choose Graystone as her intended was not only a madcap idea, but possibly a very hazardous affair. After all, what did she truly know about Lord Lane Markham Graystone?

They soon reached the aforementioned spot. The earl helped her to the bench, his firm, gloved fingers encompassing her own smaller hand. Once she was seated, Graystone propped one shoulder against the tree. He was devilishly handsome, his shoulders broad and strong. Meredith noticed that a lock of his hair had fallen down, splaying across his forehead as a breeze rustled past them.

Silence welled; a silence with which he seemed to be quite at ease, yet one that frayed Meredith's nerves. Now was the time, she knew, to voice the practiced speech she'd prepared. She'd gone over it so many times in her sitting rooms that she knew each word by heart.

Unfortunately, this moment was nothing like she'd envisioned. There was a decided distance between them, and on her own part a definite physical awareness she'd not felt nearly seven years ago. Meredith frowned.

"A penny for your thoughts," Graystone said.

Meredith shook herself from her reverie, blinked, and saw him fully, though rather blurred, once again. She had no need of her spectacles to know he was gazing at her with an intensity that was far too intimate. She suppressed the swirl of sensation that began in her stomach and threatened to blossom all throughout her body.

"I—I was thinking what a lovely day it is," she managed, and even to her own ears the reply sounded lame and silly.

"Were you?" he asked. Clearly, he guessed she'd been thinking of him.

Meredith, flustered, lowered her lashes, debating whether or not just to say what was on the tip of her tongue.

"Come now, there is something you wish to say to me, is there not?" he prompted. "We are old friends, after all."

Meredith looked up at him. His last words were spoken as a statement and yet, she could not shake the feeling he'd meant them as a question.

"Yes, my lord, we are old friends."

"Laney," he insisted. "Earlier, you addressed me as Laney." He grinned, causing Meredith to feel an uncomfortable breathlessness. "Will you not continue to do so?"

Meredith's heart warmed. Perhaps he wasn't so changed as she'd first believed.

"I will," she agreed, "when there is just the two of us about. And you must call me Meredith."

"Very well, Meredith," he replied, and on his lips her name sounded as pure as a prayer, as sweet as honey.

As Meredith looked into his green, green gaze, she was suddenly glad she'd come to the Hyde Park this day . . . and just as suddenly ready to tell Laney of her marriage agreement.

He looked into those amber eyes of hers and knew, without a doubt, that Miss Meredith Darlington had a plan of some sort. Eyes such as hers did not lie, nor did they hide the excitement mixed with hesitation she was surely feeling.

Odd, he thought, that this woman—the woman he'd known would seek him out sooner or later—could appear so fresh, and well . . . naive. It was the only term that suited her.

He had expected a female more experienced. A vixen, perhaps. At the least, he'd expected to be approached by a woman who knew well the effect her beauty had on the males she thought to deceive.

Could she be playing a game with him? No doubt she was. This innocence was surely a screen, just as was her choice of employing a nitwitted abigail. And the level-headed Lady Beveridge, how had she come into all of this? No doubt the elderly woman was merely another smokescreen who had been lured into Meredith Darlington's silken web of deceit.

He made yet another mental note to tread cautiously. He hadn't survived the waste of life's hardships by being foolish where the fairer sex was concerned. His time abroad had taught him that even the most guileless women could be agents of the enemy.

And he had a very dark and dangerous enemy dogging his trail.

One that was unknown but had proved, thus far, to be frightfully all-knowing.

He knew he must go along with this woman's game—at least until he learned the identity of the vile traitor who threatened all that was dear to him.

So thinking, he moved away from the tree, sitting down beside her. He fixed a smile on his face, gazed at her with a warmth that came with alarming ease, and said, "Tell me, Meredith, what is it you wish to say to me?"

Meredith felt a thrill at his nearness. This new Laney, so worldly and unutterably handsome, proved to be more than she'd anticipated.

But he was an old, dear friend, she reminded herself, and found comfort in the memory of how things used to be between them, and also in the fact they'd fallen into the habit of referring to each other by their given names.

Well, almost.

He hadn't addressed her as his merry Meredith. Perhaps he would soon. That he hadn't done so yet was not so very alarming, was it? she asked herself. After all, it had been almost seven years ago that they'd talked and walked and shared secrets and laughter. In time, she trusted, they'd be close friends again.

Meredith took a deep breath. Finally, she was prepared to say what was in her mind and in her heart.

But when the words came, they rushed out too fast. It couldn't be helped. How did one voice a proposal of a platonic marriage, anyway?

Meredith had no idea. She just knew she had to say it and be done with it.

She pivoted her body so that she faced him, and in her excitement, she unwittingly brushed her knees against his. She hoped he hadn't noticed her clumsiness. Hoped he would hear her out, too.

"I know this might come as a shock to you, Laney, but I can think of no other way to propose this, and so I shall just say it."

"I am listening," he replied.

She was relieved at the softness of his tone. Dear Laney. He'd always been a good listener. She hastened to continue.

"You knew my father, knew what a stickler he was for planning and plotting and forever seeing to the details of those around him, and well, he decreed that by the time I turned three-and-twenty that I should be married, and if not, that a husband should be chosen for me post-haste.

"As you can see, I am not yet wed even though my natal day is drawing near, and—," she took another deep breath, plunging ahead, "—and you of all people know that I've never fancied myself the marriageable type. I wasn't one given to romantic notions and such, and I fear I haven't changed in the least. Since my father's death, I've come to enjoy my freedom, yet I am also beholden to carrying out my father's dying wish. I do not fashion to be married to just anyone for the sake of marrying, Laney. I—I would much rather choose my husband, but I've not favored any of the gentleman who have asked for my hand, and so I came here today hoping to speak with you . . ."

Meredith paused, blushing when she hadn't meant to blush at all. She hesitated for only a moment, as tears of fear and frustration and even hope, threatened to overtake her. She rushed on before those tears could smart her eyes or constrict her throat.

"You see, Laney, if I must marry, I should like to do so with someone with whom I am at ease, can trust and with whom I am friends," she said softly. "I—I would like to marry *you.*"

There. She'd said it! God in heaven help her, but she'd said it.

Meredith caught her lower lip between her teeth, her whole body trembling, as she watched and waited, and wondered if he would laugh in her face.

He couldn't believe what he was hearing. Of all the things he thought she'd say, this wasn't it. Not by far.

Marriage? Gad, she was bold!

Marriage! To her, his enemy's spy and confidante? And that she would dare claim they'd been friends, that she had known him so well once upon a time—it was all too unbelievable!

And yet . . . he could swear he saw true tears beginning to pool in those entrancing amber eyes of hers, and her tone was heartbreakingly honest, even a tad choked, as though she were speaking past a heartfelt lump in her throat.

Damme, but she was good.

If he hadn't known better, he'd have believed every word she uttered.

But she wasn't true or truthful or even a tadbit trustworthy.

She was the enemy. Or close enough to it. He must queer her game, but never, ever, let her know he was doing so.

He quelled the tightness gathering in his jaw, forced himself not to call her out for the deceitful creature he knew her to be.

"Marriage, Meredith?" he asked, still thunderstruck but not alluding to that fact.

She nodded, quickly. Her eyes were wide and sweetly moist in her heart-shaped face. He noticed her fists were clenched tight together upon her lap.

He thought it best to play along, soothe her, encourage her even. He reached for her hands, covering the soft kid of her gloves with his own.

"Why me, Meredith?" he asked quietly. She trembled beneath his touch, surprising him with that reaction.

"Oh, Laney," she whispered, truly seeming to agonize over her words, "I think you know why. You once told me the two of us were cut of the same cloth. Neither of us had any mind to marry back then, but you knew that eventually you must marry, once you ascended your title, and you told me you hoped to find a woman who had little need of romance or pretty phrases, but one who would be happy enough to go her own way as you went yours. You said yourself you wished for a *platonic* marriage, that you sought not a—a lover—," and here she blushed magnificently, "—but rather a companion with whom you could share your books and your thoughts . . ."

She smiled, tremulously. "I have grown to be such a woman, Laney. I—I am not the sort who needs a man to make everything right in my world. Indeed, I too wish for someone with whom I can be at ease and not worry about the—the romantic illusions most brides have of marriage."

She looked directly at him. The amber lights blazed in her gaze as she said, very sincerely, "I believe, Laney,

I am the kind of wife you desire. I would never be affronted if you chose to spend your evenings pouring over your ledgers and books. I do not need the excitement of parties or gatherings. Nor do I need coddling or constant attention. You would be free to do as you pleased, and I—I would be free to do the same. I think it would be a famous arrangement."

Famous? he thought. It sounded like sheer hell! Imagine, marrying such a beautiful woman and not claiming her body every night but instead choosing ledgers and books. Egad, what a total waste of a marriage *that* would be.

And what a supreme pity, too, for Meredith Darlington, whether she was sinner or saint, was made for a man's pleasure. She, with her bewitching eyes and generous curves, her unwittingly sensuous nature and her sweet voice, was not the type of female a man could ever ignore. To marry her would be to bed her nightly, to always and forever make her totally and thoroughly his own. There was no possible way that *he* would ever agree to a platonic marriage with such a female.

But, of course, she wasn't asking *him*.

She was beseeching a man she thought to be the rightful third Earl of Graystone—which he would have been, had he been born into the world three minutes earlier than his twin.

As it was, he hadn't been. He'd come second into the world, following his brother, and had remained in the shadows, at least in their father's eyes, ever since.

He wasn't the true and rightful heir to the Graystone title, though he'd taken on that guise. In truth, he was the black sheep of the family, the ne'er-do-well son, and a man who would not hesitate to take an eye for an eye.

The beautiful Miss Meredith Darlington, whether she knew it or not—and he suspected she did!—had proposed a marriage of convenience to the wrong brother.

Five

Meredith realized, mortified, that she was feeling breathless and her heart was beating unnaturally fast, yet she knew it wasn't wholly her bold proposal that was making her feel this way.

It was Laney.

Or rather, the man Laney had become; disturbingly handsome, quietly certain of himself and his place in the world.

And she was attracted to him.

She shouldn't be. Attraction of this nature had no place in her plan. More so, he wouldn't be pleased should he ever know of it.

Guilt overcame her as she looked away, unable to hold his gaze for a moment longer.

"I—I feel foolish and embarrassed," she murmured. "Pray, forgive me, and do you forget I have even uttered the words I have."

She rose to her feet, intending to leave.

"Meredith."

She stilled at the sound of his voice, so deep and sounding far more enchanting than Laney's voice had ever sounded to her ears.

She turned her face slightly, seeing from beneath the brim of her bonnet that he, too, had gotten to his feet.

He stood tall and strong just behind her. She noted that a shaft of sunlight struck his face, turning his beryl-colored eyes to green fire.

"Yes?"

"I would have you look at me fully when I say this."

He was going to decline her proposal. Meredith felt her heart fall. Oh, but she'd been silly and reckless and too much caught up in what she'd remembered from a summer that had happened long ago. She should have known better. He was a titled lord now, no longer the Laney who'd befriended her.

Feeling as though she was turning to face a sentence of doom, Meredith pivoted, lifted her face, and prepared herself for a lowering set-down.

He didn't smile at her, nor did he frown. He merely gazed long and hard at her. When he finally spoke, he asked, "Old friends can never lie to each other, true?"

Slowly, Meredith nodded, swallowing past the tightness in her throat. She tried very hard to act as though it would not crush her were he to say no. Indeed, she prayed she appeared very cool and composed, which she wasn't.

"And since we are old friends," he continued, almost carefully, "I trust you will not take offense when I say I would like some time to ponder what you have proposed. Too, I think we should discuss this in greater detail. Not here and not now, though." His gaze not leaving hers, he motioned with just a nod of his head to the area behind her. "Your abigail," he explained, "is approaching. She's found not only her shoe, but the two of us as well."

Meredith would have turned to look then save for the

fact that she felt like a moth to the flame in Laney's gaze. She felt herself hypnotized by those green pools.

"We will meet again, somewhere other than the busy paths of Hyde Park," he told her.

Before she could think, the word was out of her mouth: "When?"

If he noticed her anticipation, he made no show of it. "Soon."

Betsy was just behind Meredith then, and there came the sure sounds of carriages moving freely along the lane once again. There was no longer any reason for Meredith and Laney to linger in the park.

He escorted her back to the lane.

Before she knew it, Meredith was seated beside Peach again, Boyle had clicked his team into motion, the wind was in her face . . . and the third Earl of Graystone was somewhere behind her.

"Tell all," whispered Peach, gazing at Meredith. "Did you or didn't you? Say what you'd wished to say to him, that is."

Meredith sat back, feeling ridiculously dreamy-eyed, and yet confused as well. "I did," she replied.

"And?" Peach pressed.

"He listened."

"But did he give you an *answer,* my dear Merry?"

Meredith thought of her time in the park with the new Laney—for that is how she thought of him now; the "new" Laney.

"Alas, no," she replied, shaking her head.

Peach pursed her lips, tut-tutting. "I warned you away from him, Meredith. Truly, I wish you would forget this ridiculous notion of yours. The man, such as he is now, will crush your heart, I am certain of it, and if I were you I would put him out of my mind and—"

"Peach," Meredith said, interrupting her friend, "he did not break my heart."

"You just said he didn't give you an answer. That, in my estimation, clearly bodes ill for your plans, my dear."

"You don't understand," Meredith murmured. "I—I am to meet with him again. He has promised to seek me out, somewhere, at some time." Even as she said the words, Meredith was unable to hide the expectation in her voice, or the nervousness in her limbs. She felt herself tremble at the mere idea of being alone with Laney once again.

Peach, noting Meredith's physical reaction, tut-tutted again. "Well," she muttered, and then, seemingly at a loss for words, settled back against the squabs, adding, "well, well, well." She gave Meredith a pointed stare, and said, "You will tell me later about how you and his lordship are acquainted. I should like to know. I'd also like to know why you hadn't mentioned that fact to me sooner."

Meredith assured her friend she would explain things. How much she would explain, though, Meredith had not yet decided.

Betsy, having listened intently to the exchange, and never one to keep quiet in spite of her station in life, said, "Oooh, Miss Merry, how exciting! His lordship might pop up when you least expect him! Or mayhap he'll come calling with a posy and a poem! Or maybe—"

Peach gave the girl a quelling look. "For once in your life, Betsy, do hush."

"Yes, ma'am," Betsy said, dropping her lashes. And then, unable to help herself, she lifted her beaming face to Meredith, adding in a fast whisper, "Or mayhap he'll just simply come some night and sweep you away to Gretna Green! Imagine, eloping with the likes of his lordship!"

"Betsy!" Meredith exclaimed.

"Oh, coo, Miss Merry, but *anything* could happen! He is so handsome and mysterious, and nothing like I've heard you paint him as being. Now that I've seen him in the flesh, I can't picture him as the shy man you've talked about. He *is* changed. And excitingly dangerous."

Meredith wanted to inform her maid that she *shouldn't* be saying so, but of course Meredith had never been one to work overly hard at insisting her servants keep their tongues in check. She'd enjoyed their closeness and had on too many times to count encouraged them to speak their minds.

Now, however, she regretted such an outlandish habit. Peach, seated beside her, seemed to agree with Meredith as she gave the maid a frown.

Betsy, lips forming a pout, finally sat back. She did, however, dare a bold and conspiratorial wink in Meredith's direction. Before she became totally subdued, she whispered, "I think, Miss Merry, that losing your bonnet to his lordship was the wisest thing you've ever done."

Meredith did not tell her maid that she'd lost not only her bonnet that day . . . but perhaps her heart as well.

And yet the Laney she'd walked with and talked with was nothing like the Laney she remembered so vividly. No. He was something more, something totally and un-utterably more.

The person he'd become had been unexpected and, dash it all, a flame to the kindling of her heart.

Larkin watched as the marriageable Miss Meredith's carriage drew out of sight. He had been puzzled by her seeming honesty during her proposal in the park, but he was not so careless as to believe her. Pretty faces and pretty words had never proved to lead him astray in the past, and he wasn't about to let that happen now.

So she was beautiful. It was of no consequence. So she blushed and became shy at the proper moment. What practiced female couldn't, especially when the price was high enough?

He climbed up onto the bench of his high-perched phaeton, taking the ribbons from his ever-ready groom, slapped his spirited team into motion, and was glad to feel the wind slice through his teeth as he headed out of Hyde Park at an alarming speed.

He had much to ponder.

Later, Larkin headed for White's, for an early dinner and for the solace of his only trusted friend in this dangerous game he'd begun.

He found Sir Harry Drake seated at the table Drake had often sat at with Laney in the time following the end of the war. Larkin and Drake shared a meal and some drink as well.

"You are troubled, I think," Drake commented much later, a concerned look in his brown eyes. "In fact, you haven't said more than two words since you sat down. Care to bend my ear about it?"

"I have experienced the oddest of afternoons," Larkin said.

"I s'pose they've all been odd since you've returned. What makes today any different, old friend?"

"A female."

"There's always a female where you are concerned. Do not tell me some lovely London lady has captured your heart."

Larkin frowned, contemplating the port in his glass. "If my guess is correct, this one is no lady. Only pretending to be." He glanced up. "Tell me what you know about one Meredith Darlington."

Drake sat back, his smile fading as he let out a soft whistle through his teeth. "Miss Darlington? *She* is the one who has affected you so?"

"You know of her?"

"Most definitely," said Drake. "As has any man who has his sights set to marrying. She's an heiress. Resides in Russell Square. Her father was a banker, one of the Darlington Three. You've heard of them, no doubt."

Larkin gave a vague nod. "I believe so," he said.

"Each of them made an enormous fortune in their banking endeavors. They were famous for not only their wise investments but their quarrels amongst each other and, of course, the lovely daughters they begat. Had one girl-child apiece, they did, and found the most unorthodox of women to be godmama to them. The young ladies are known as 'Those Darlington Cousins,' each one original, beautiful, and intelligent in her own right. Their mothers all died young and tragic deaths. The Darlington Three stayed together long enough to amass a tidy fortune and then each went their separate way with their treasured daughters in tow. The eldest, Mirabella, married the Earl of Blackwood. The youngest, Marcie, became Lord Sherringham's marchioness in what is said to be one of the most beautiful weddings."

"And Meredith?" asked Larkin.

"She has yet to choose a husband. Seems to like her freedom. For those of the *ton* who do not scorn to lower themselves by marrying the daughter of a tradesman, she is quite a catch. Her father left her a dizzying sum of money, but for whatever reason, made certain she could touch no more of it than the income from her inheritance. Her trustees control the capital. Word has it, though, Miss Darlington is determined to take complete control of her fortune. Problem is, her trustees won't relinquish that control until she is married."

"So why hasn't she gone to the altar yet?"

"Can't say as I know. She's certainly had enough offers."

Larkin grunted. "Doubtless only from the riffraff of the *ton* who've fallen into dun territory and have no more pursestrings to pull within their own families."

"There have been those," Drake admitted. "But there have been as many honest offers for her hand. Miss Darlington, though you think otherwise, appears to be every inch a lady and a pleasant one at that. Even though she is the daughter of a banker, the doors of Society have been flung open to her. She's even scaled the walls of that exclusive club known simply as Minerva's, and has been known to attend meetings of the secretive Midnight Society. Not only that, but she's made a true friend in the esteemable Lady Peach Beveridge, one of Minerva's and the Midnight Society's founders. All in all, there seems to be nothing to blight the young woman's good character."

Larkin, digesting all of this information, was not totally convinced Miss Meredith Darlington was what she appeared to be. She'd been hiding some truth from him while in the Park. He was certain of it. But *what?*

"Miss Darlington sought me out this day, Drake," he said. "Claimed she'd known me—or rather, that she'd known my brother," he added in a whisper.

"Perhaps she did know your brother," Drake offered, his voice just as low.

"You don't understand. She came seeking a *marriage*. Muttered some such nonsense about the two of us—of *them*—being very close friends in the past. Good Lord, but I can't remember my brother ever mentioning her name! Yet what a tale she spun, about the two of them being thick as thieves and a lot of other fuddled notions!"

"Perhaps," Drake suggested, "Miss Darlington spoke the truth when she claimed she knew such a close bond with you . . . er . . . with Laney."

Larkin let out a harsh breath. "I think Miss Darlington is playing me for a fool. In fact, I wouldn't be surprised if she is a pawn in my enemy's deadly game."

"A preposterous notion, surely! Miss Darlington's reputation is impeccable, old friend. Her only blemish, thus far, has been merely the fact she is the daughter of a tradesman, nothing more."

"But what," demanded Larkin, "do you truly know of her?"

Drake paused. "Not much," he finally admitted after a moment of consideration. "Only that she comes and goes from the City. She seems to like to travel, as do her cousins. They've been reared to consider all the world as theirs for the taking. She was in France for a time before she traveled to Cornwall to visit her cousin, Marcie."

Larkin lifted one brow.

"Now don't go painting her black just because she stepped on French soil," Drake said. "The reason she traveled there is because she sought to end some of her father's previous investments. She is a very astute female, I've heard tell."

"Either that," Larkin said darkly, "or she is a spy among us, a conspirator with the person who wants me dead. Perhaps she is the blonde-haired messenger who spoke with that river rat, Bart. And mayhap, the man she conspires with is someone I knew from my days in France."

Drake leaned back in his chair, blowing out a slow whistle. "Good God, I'd never have even thought of all that. If this is true, what do you plan to do?"

"The only thing I can."

"Which is?"

"Queer her game by seriously considering her suggestion of marriage."

Drake paled at the significance of Larkin's words. "And if she isn't the deceitful female you think her to be? What then, my friend?"

"I'll have made a mistake."

"You could break her heart," Drake cautioned.

"Only if I am wrong, which I don't believe I am."

"And what of your brother? Have you thought of *him*, of what pain it might bring him, if indeed he still lives, and if he and Miss Darlington were as close as she claims?"

Larkin's knuckles turned white around the glass he held in his hand. "My brother *is* alive, dammit. Never doubt that, do you hear me? *Never.*"

"Easy now," Drake soothed in a low whisper. "I hear you. And I, too, hope it is true, but all we found that night on the docks, and for several after that, was a woman reeking of gin who claimed that she'd seen a man, the very likeness of you, being carted off by some sailors and bleeding from a gunshot wound. If it was Laney—which I think it was—then he suffered a serious injury. We have no clue as to what happened to him after that. The both of us went with little sleep for weeks while we turned the city inside out, and still found nothing. Even the trained investigators you've hired to continuously scour the waterfront have found no signs of him, and—"

"My brother isn't dead," Larkin interrupted with a snap. "If he were, I would know it. I'd . . . oh damme," he breathed, his anger dissipating. "Just trust me, Drake. If my brother were dead, I would know. I'd *feel* it here . . . in my heart."

Drake let out a slow breath, having gone over and over Laney's disappearance with Larkin more times than he cared to count. He knew how much Larkin wanted to believe the best where Laney was concerned. And truth be told, Drake did not totally feel Laney's absence—at least, not the way he had felt the moment Amabel met her demise, and Drake hadn't been anywhere near Amabel at that time. He knew what Larkin meant about "feeling" Laney's loss.

"Very well," Drake finally said. "Your brother *is* alive . . . and now you've encountered Miss Darlington. She, as well as all of the *ton,* believe you are someone you're not. What do you think to gain from this subterfuge?"

"The truth," Larkin breathed. "I intend to ferret out the murderous villain who thought to end not only my life but my brother's as well." He stared hard at Drake. "I've the feeling Miss Darlington is connected to the culprit."

"You go too far! 'Tis a reckless notion."

"I am a reckless man, Drake. I always have been."

Drake leaned forward against the table. "No, my friend, what you are is wounded in your soul and bitter in your heart. You came back to London, guised as your brother, because you are too stubborn and too guilt-ridden over what happened in the past between you two. You don't want him to be missing or hurt or even dead. You want Laney alive . . . and so now he *is* alive—at least to the *ton*—because you've slipped into his boots and his mannerisms. But mark my words, you are playing with fire by thinking to outfox your enemy by allowing him to think you are dead and that he fouled his attempt in murdering Laney. Too, you are foolish to court a woman who might very well be the love of Laney's youth."

A storm gathered in Larkin's gaze. "If it were anyone but you to say such things to me, I would call the fool out."

"And no doubt be the victor—with anyone but me, that is," replied Drake with a small smile. "But I care about you . . . bloody hell, Larkin, I love you like a son. I hate seeing you create such a tangled web, especially with your brother's life, a life you've stepped into and won't easily be able to step out of. You've become moody and guarded these past few weeks." He settled back in the chair once again. "I know you, friend. I know what a surly, bristly sort you can be. I also know the fine, sensitive fellow who resides beneath that chilling facade of yours. You've a heart of gold beneath all the ice that has crusted about you. I'd like to see the goodness in you once again."

Larkin mellowed a bit in the face of Drake's words.

"You're a fine man, Drake," he acknowledged. "A good friend."

Drake, who knew that Larkin never said anything but what he truly felt, grinned at the words. "I try to be. But it's deuced hard at times with a bitter soul such as yours."

"I have a right to be bitter," Larkin reminded him.

"You did," corrected Drake. "Once. But your father is dead now."

"Some wounds never heal, old friend, especially in the absence of filial love." Larkin suddenly raked one hand through his rich, coppery hair. "Gad," he breathed, "I am surrounded by memories in this city, few of them good, and I can't help but feel as though the wretched man who was my father, is reaching out from his grave to twist a noose about my neck."

"What are you saying?"

Larkin's eyes narrowed. "Whoever hired the thugs to attack us, and another to shoot Laney, is someone from my past . . . someone who hates me as much my father did. I won't rest until I know the truth of what happened to Laney, and I won't stop until I unveil the hideous being who caused my brother's disappearance. The villain won't be able to hide for long. I intend to make him pay, Drake. If it takes me the rest of my life, I'm going to see that he pays."

"I was afraid you'd say that."

Larkin ignored Drake's comment. "If the marriageable Miss Darlington has anything to do with him, then I shall uncover her for the deceitful being she is. I'll stop at nothing to find and then protect my brother. Do you hear? *Nothing.* Not even marrying some Cit's daughter."

"Yet Miss Darlington is not just some 'Cit's daughter,' but the cherished offspring of a man who was wealthy as a king and just as influential during his lifetime. To bring the lady heartache or dishonor will not go unheeded by those who adore the woman. And I warn you now, she is adored by many, my friend."

"You mean the *ton*," Larkin said, and the word was like acid on his tongue.

"Exactly. To do her wrong might be to bring a blight upon your own family name."

Larkin leaned forward. "To the devil with the name, Drake, it is my brother I'm worried about. I have not returned to London to play a puppet that will do and say the right things. I've come to find and protect Laney, and to put my own mind at ease."

"So you say, but you seem to be forgetting one thing. The *ton* and their haughty opinions are very dear to your brother. Indeed, they are everything to him. To play your hand lightly will undoubtedly cast your brother in an unfavorable light should he soon surface. The boots you walk in now aren't your own, Larkin. Never forget that. Though you despise parties and poetry, simpering females and senseless small talk, your brother has long embraced all of these things, and now so, too, must you."

"And I will—but I don't have to like it," Larkin said.

"You alone are the one who began this masquerade. You've begun the game and now must play it out. You've no one to blame but yourself."

"Wrong. I blame my enemy, Drake."

"But it is your brother's sterling character, and even Miss Darlington's gentle heart, you are putting at risk."

Larkin's expression turned grave. What his friend said was true enough, dammit all.

"As always, Drake, you are correct. I'll do well to heed your advice."

Drake frowned. "Hell, my friend, you'd fare far better to just forget this deadly vendetta you have with a man you can't even name. But I don't suppose there's any chance of that, eh?"

"No," said Larkin.

"Then at least remember not to storm any castles your brother wouldn't," Drake warned. "As for Miss Darlington, I'd tread carefully were I you. Who knows? Maybe Laney *had* romanced her."

And maybe he hadn't, thought Larkin, knowing his brother had never been one to chase after skirts.

"I shouldn't alienate her, were I you," advised Drake, finished with his sermon.

Their talk turned to other things then. Later, they shared some brandy after their dinner, but not even the brandy could ease Larkin's troubled thoughts. He declined to join Drake in one of the outer rooms for a game of chance, heading out into the unseasonably cool night air instead.

The enigma the marriageable Miss Meredith had presented was beginning to overtake his every thought. He found it difficult to forget her intriguing amber eyes and the fact he'd known she was concealing some truth from him. It was a secret she hadn't want him—or perhaps Laney—to know about.

What could that secret be?

Larkin decided he would take Drake's advice not to "storm any castles." Instead, he would take his time in getting to know Miss Meredith Darlington. He'd seek her out, find her and approach her at the most unexpected moments. He'd make her think their meetings were unplanned. He'd be natural and unimposing, would draw her into conversation with alarming ease. He would be pleasant, chatty, charming, even flirtatious.

If she was his enemy's cohort, he would eventually reveal that fact, then he'd make her pay for such deceit.

And if she wasn't connected to his enemy?

Larkin chose not to think of that possibility. Meredith Darlington obviously had some plan afoot.

No doubt that plan meant trouble.

She couldn't possibly be some innocent from Laney's past. Not by far.

Six

After leaving Hyde Park, Meredith spent the remainder of that afternoon, the following night, and the early next morning as well, nervously anticipating the moment when she would again meet with Laney. But when he didn't come calling or even send so much as his card, she wondered again if her time with him had been nothing more than a hopeful dream.

She decided it was silly to wait for him, and even sillier to think she'd made some sort of impression upon him with her unorthodox proposal. Obviously, this new Laney was not so indulgent of his friendships as he'd been in the past. Doubtless he had many matters to attend.

Or perhaps he did not intend to continue their conversation at all. What if he'd only said he would see her again when in fact he'd not meant to do so at all? What if—?

No, she could not continue this line of thinking or in another moment she would lose all hope. She must harbor only optimistic thoughts. Laney was the man she wished to marry, and she *would* marry him.

Deciding not to stay at home and fidget, Meredith chose to go out. She'd promised to take Peach's niece, Julianne, round to the modistes this day and she herself had hoped to stop at the lending library before they began their shopping expedition.

After sending word to Julianne of her imminent arrival, she ordered her carriage to be brought around. Within the half-hour, Boyle and his team were waiting for Meredith and her abigail beyond the stoop. The late morning was bright and beautiful, and once they'd retrieved Julianne from her residence, the three of them sat back and enjoyed the sunshine.

Julianne, Meredith decided, was not the plain Jane Society had painted her as being. There was a true sincerity in her pale blue eyes, and Meredith knew that if the young woman would take more of an interest in her dressing habits, she could very well become a lovely swan.

However, the sad fact was, though, that at twenty years of age, Julianne had yet to capture any gentleman's interest, even though she'd had several Seasons. It was a shame her parents had sequestered her in the country with an aged and uninspiring governess for so many years for the young woman seemed to be at a loss in Town. She'd even begun to think of herself as "on the shelf," as too many gentleman of the *ton* obviously thought her to be. Julianne had resigned herself to a life void of matrimony.

The young woman's mother, when she thought to consider Julianne at all, saw her only as a telling marker of her own aging self. As for Julianne's scholarly father, he much preferred to hole himself up in his library with his heavy texts of ancient Hebrew and not bother himself with his shy offspring.

Julianne's mother had made arrangements to send Julianne back to the country (and had clearly decided to keep the young woman there for good!) while she herself headed to Brighton for the summer. Peach, however, had stepped in and insisted Julianne stay with her.

Peach had decided to take the girl under her wing. Meredith had thought it a good idea and had made every effort to include Julianne in her own plans. She thought the girl would have enjoyed a summer in Brighton, but knew better than to believe Julianne's mother would pay much mind to the young woman there.

Today, as with any other day, Julianne was not much in the mood for a shopping expedition. Her thoughts were not on silks and ribands but rather books, and when Meredith mentioned she'd like to browse a bit at the library, Julianne suddenly came alive.

"What a perfect suggestion!" said Julianne. "I would like to borrow some of Shakespeare's sonnets. And perhaps we could stop at a bookstore where I can purchase a volume of Lord Byron's poetry?" Julianne clapped her gloved hands together, positively beaming.

Meredith, though she'd been asked by Peach to try and stir the girl's interest in fashions, could not deny a fellow reader the heady delight of a bookstore or two.

"I think that is a marvelous idea," said Meredith.

She gave orders for her coachman to take them first to the lending library. Meredith determined to choose for herself a good book in which she could find a few hours to forget about her own predicament with Laney, and hoped to allow Julianne time enough to immerse herself in Shakespeare's moving sonnets. In two days' time there was to be a small card-party at the home of Lady Darcy, who had returned early from her stay in Bath and was hoping to round up a few of those who now resided in the Capital for some light entertainment. Julianne,

Meredith knew, did not wish to attend the card-party and had agreed to do so only for her aunt's sake. Knowing this, Meredith thought to cheer Julianne with some book shopping. And so it was that they headed for the lending library.

The library was not overly crowded. A few people were reading the papers, others browsing the bookshelves. Julianne immediately headed for her beloved sonnets while Meredith wove her own way through the maze of shelves. Betsy, ever curious and nosy, chose to stand nearer to the door and "people watch" as she called it.

Meredith, at the back of one stall, came upon an old novel penned a century before that was not at all what a lady should read. It was a thundering tale of blood feuds and furious revenge, complete with a mustache-twirling villain and a hero who was a nobleman turned outlaw and seemed to enjoy slicing his enemies down to size.

The hero, oddly enough, reminded her somewhat of the new Laney.

Though not at all intended for the fair sex, the story proved to be the perfect remedy for Meredith's restlessness. By the second chapter, she was engagingly hooked.

She rather liked the hero, who became an outlaw because he did not fashion allowing the poor of the land to grow poorer while the rich grew richer. Pity that the heroine the man chose was a female much given to histrionics, a lady with a grating habit of screaming or fainting at the most inopportune moments. As for any other female in the tale, they all proved to be scheming, devious creatures who would as soon lure a man to doom than smile at him. Meredith, her spectacles now perched on her nose, allowed herself to be caught up in the story anyway.

She did not look up when someone came down the aisle in which she was standing, and she barely noticed when that same person moved behind her. The hero was just about to dispense with yet another enemy when Meredith heard someone speak to her. Of a sudden, she had the sensation that same someone was reading over her shoulder the words of the book she'd chosen.

"I should think," came a soft, low voice, "you would choose to read something with less violence and perhaps more romance."

Startled, Meredith turned. "Laney!" she whispered.

"Good morning, Meredith."

She stood with her back to the bookcase, feeling dwarfed by the rugged and very broad-shouldered third Earl of Graystone. For once, Meredith was glad she wore her spectacles for she could now clearly see his startling handsomeness. Not even the semi-darkness of the library could hide the brilliance of his green eyes and the fineness of his features.

Meredith felt dull in comparison. And her spectacles, blast them, were sliding down the bridge of her nose as they so often did. She reached up, intending to remove them.

"Ah, no," he said softly. "I'd rather you kept them on." He gently pushed them to their proper place, as though he'd been doing the deed for years. "You look very pretty in your spectacles, Meredith."

Meredith blinked. "Thank you," she murmured, not knowing how to react in the face of such familiarity; just yesterday she'd have sworn he hadn't remembered her at all!

Graystone smiled. "Borrowing a book, I see. May I?" he asked, even as he reached out to tip it up slightly so that he could see the title on the spine of its marbled cover.

"Hmmm," he commented, "were I have gone on a quest to gift you with a book, I fear I would not have chosen this particular one. If it is excitement you enjoy in your literature maybe you should consider the works of George Gordon."

Meredith found her voice. "I have read Lord Byron, and am pleased with his works. But I am not given to restricting my reading to one type of literature only."

"You are adventurous in your choices of reading then?" At her nod, he asked, "And in life, Meredith? Does the same hold true?"

"What a ridiculous question," she answered without thinking. "You know me, Laney. You know—" Meredith stopped her spate of words, feeling her face color. She would have snapped her mouth shut and said no more if not for the fact he clearly awaited an answer. "I suppose I have an adventurous heart," she admitted. "All we Darlington women do. And there are those who claim I am a bit too spirited at times and . . . and reckless in my choices, I suppose." *But you know all of that, Laney. You know all about my reckless side,* she thought to herself.

He motioned to the book in her hands with a nod of his head. "Tell me, Meredith, what character in this novel has intrigued you most thus far? The villain with all his shades of gray and poisonous plans? Or is it perhaps the lovely Adorinda who isn't so lovely come the end of the tale when she is discovered to be a spy?"

Meredith sensed her answer was important to him, but could not fathom why it should be. Nor could she understand his change of mood since yesterday. In Hyde Park, she'd had the distinct impression she'd surprised Laney by reminding him of their past, and she knew for a fact she'd most certainly taken him aback with her bold idea of a marriage betwixt them.

Yet here he was, a part of him still keenly reminding her of the Laney she'd known . . . and the other half of him being very *un*like the Laney she remembered. Meredith could make neither heads or tails of it, so decided to simply cease dissecting the situation.

"Shame on you, Laney, for revealing the end of the story to me," she said. "I will not be able to finish the book for I now know how it ends."

"But I haven't told you the end, not really. Only that the female spy is uncovered. I haven't told you how or when or even by whom. Most important," he said softly, "I did not reveal what happens to her after that."

Meredith closed the book. "I can well imagine," she said, turning slightly to replace the novel on the shelf. "Doubtless the woman suffers disgrace and later a slow and hideous death at the hands of the hero." She returned her gaze to his. "He, by the way, is the one."

"I beg your pardon?" Graystone said.

"The lord turned outlaw; he is the character who has intrigued me the most. You did ask."

He went perfectly still. "Yes," he murmured. "I did ask." He gazed at her intently.

There came a motion from the end of the long bookcase. It was Julianne, with Betsy behind her. Julianne had chosen her book and was now giving a tiny wave of her hand to Meredith. And Betsy, blast her, was craning her neck, peering over Julianne's shoulder and grinning from ear to ear.

Meredith returned her gaze to Laney's. "I—I must be going," she said.

Noticing her companions, he nodded. "Of course," he said.

Meredith felt a moment of pique. A part of her wished he had instead insisted she stay longer. Long enough, anyway, to give her his answer of whether or not he would consider her plan of marriage. But he hadn't. Instead, he played the genteel gentleman, bowing slightly, and then taking his leave of her.

Meredith watched as he walked away . . . and marveled at the fact that she'd sensed he was "playing" the part of a genteel gentleman. But why should she think such a thing? Laney *was* a gentleman. Always had been.

And yet . . . Meredith could not convince herself that he was not enacting a role he believed she expected him to play. How odd that she should think such a thing! Even so, there was something that rang false about the Earl of Graystone.

But what, exactly, was it about him that wasn't true?

Meredith, unfortunately, had no idea. She only knew there was something wholly different about the man. Something he did not want her to know.

Meredith headed toward her abigail and Julianne. In spite of herself she looked for Lord Graystone among the patrons of the library as she and Julianne went through the motions of borrowing their chosen books.

Laney, though, was gone.

Seven

Meredith sat in the sunny breakfast parlour of her home in Russell Square, reading through the morning's post as she sipped coffee from a delicate Sevres cup and took an occasional bite of the delicately buttered toast the parlor maid had prepared for her.

The morning's mail was filled with invitations, a few matters of business, a long letter from her cousin, Marcie, and a package from Laney.

She quickly opened the package, pleased to find the opening cantos of Byron's *Childe Harold's Pilgrimage* first published sometime ago. Laney's attached note, written on a small square of vellum, was brief but made her heart skip a beat nonetheless:

For you. Yours, L.

Meredith sat for long moments staring at his bold, decisive handwriting. It was so like Laney to send her a gift of words, especially since he'd found her at the lending library yesterday, and also because they'd both been voracious readers during the summer long ago. Perhaps there was nothing false about him, mayhap she had just been unsettled by his closeness during their moments in the library, Meredith decided.

But his note . . . there was something about it that did not seem in keeping with her memories of the Laney of

her youth. He'd written to her several times at the start
of the tour upon which he'd embarked following their
summer holiday together, and Meredith had kept every
letter. She'd rolled them up tying them with ribbon, and,
at least for that first year or so, had read them again and
again.

Thinking of those letters, she knew instantly why this
brief missive seemed different. Laney had always signed
his name with a flourish; not simply with just the first
letter of his given name. And he had always begun his
notes with *To my merry Meredith.*

Nostalgia overtook her then, and she smiled, perhaps
a bit ruefully as she stared down at the single L which
wasn't widely looped at the top and bottom as Laney
had been wont to write it in the past. This L was capped
with a very small loop at the top and then a large, sweeping one at its base.

Even his handwriting was different, she thought. It
would take some time getting accustomed to this new
Laney.

Meredith was pulled out of her reverie when Stubbins,
her aged but still-sprightly and ever trustworthy butler,
announced an early morning caller.

It was none other than Peach, whom Meredith had
been expecting.

"Do show Lady Beveridge in," said Meredith. "And
do you prepare yourself for a mission this day, Stubbins.
Lady Beveridge and I shall be penning yet another missive we hope you will deliver."

Stubbins gave a quick bow and nod. "Of course, Miss
Darlington. I am ever at your service."

"Indeed you are," said Meredith, smiling. She adored
the old man. She'd known him all of her life and a little

less than half of his. It had been Stubbins who'd announced her birth to her father, and it had been Stubbins who'd given her the news of her father's death. He had been near for every milestone of her life, and he was like a great oak that might be buffeted by strong winds but could never be snapped in two.

That was the reason Meredith entrusted him with the many missives she and her friends of the Midnight Society penned. Stubbins might be getting on in his years, but he was diligent in the tasks the Society asked of him.

He showed Lady Beveridge into the parlour, then closed the doors quietly behind her, prepared to stand in wait for when his mistress would call upon him.

Meredith rose to greet her friend.

"Never you mind," said Peach, peeling off her gloves and removing her bonnet as she swept into the room. "Just stay where you are. No need to get up, and don't you dare ring for your parlor maid. I cannot stomach food before noon, as you know. But I do believe I shall have some coffee. It smells divine."

So saying, Peach moved to the sideboard and the silver coffee service there, helping herself. Meredith sat down once again, watching as Peach ladened a cup with an inordinate amount of cream and sugar.

Peach turned about, eyeing the pile of morning's post upon a silver salver near Meredith. "Any good news to be had?" she asked.

"The usual," Meredith replied. "A letter from Marcie, too many invitations . . . and, oh yes, a note from Lord Graystone."

Peach lifted one brow as she moved toward the table. "And could the latter be the same you're holding so closely to you?"

Meredith realized then she was still clutching Laney's brief missive, having pressed it against the place where her heart beat beneath her breastbone. "Yes, I guess it is."

"Hmmm," was all Peach said as she took a seat. After a moment of quiet, she asked, "When were you going to tell me, dear Merry, that you and his lordship had already made each other's acquaintance?"

Meredith felt a moment of guilt. "I'd meant to mention it. Truly I did."

"But you did not, which leads me to believe you have far deeper feelings for the man than I had at first surmised."

"Is that how it seems?" Meredith asked, somewhat amazed for she hadn't really thought about Laney in a romantic sense, at least not since she'd been sixteen and extremely impressionable. "I care about him, yes . . . but I view him mostly as a very dear friend."

Peach did not appear convinced, but she indulged her. "Go on," the older woman said softly.

Meredith sighed, placing Laney's note on the silver salver with the other post. "We met when my father and I spent a summer holiday at Graystone Manor. I had just celebrated my sixteenth birthday and the world was just opening up to me, or so it seemed. Laney was one-and-twenty and about to embark on a tour. I think for him, as well, the world appeared wide and wonderful. We spent a great deal of time talking and sharing hopes and such." Meredith smiled, remembering.

"You fell in love with him," Peach said.

"Perhaps the young girl in me did . . . but that isn't why I've now chosen him as the man I wish to marry, not totally."

"What is the reason, my dear?" Peach gently asked.

Meredith hesitated, but she knew her friend deserved an answer—and truth be known, Meredith suddenly wished to share her secret with Peach. "I have never told another soul about this, but I know you do not approve of my choice in Laney and so I shall share this story with you in hopes you will understand my reasons."

"You have my ear, my dear, and my solemn vow that what you tell me now will never be repeated."

Quietly, Meredith began her story. "There was one particular night at the beginning of that holiday when I could not sleep, so I went out riding, alone. It was a foolish and reckless thing to do, but the moon beckoned me and I loved the feel of the wind in my face. That's when I saw Laney. He rode toward me, astride a lathered horse. He'd thought not to be noticed returning home well after midnight and certainly hadn't expected to find *me* greeting him at the gates to Graystone.

"His hair had been tossed about by the wind and his eyes were so filled with life that I knew instantly he, too, found freedom in a wild night's ride. We took our time returning to the stables, talking about everything, about nothing. It was the most magical experience.

"The next day the constable arrived. He was in an irritated mood for someone fitting Laney's description had been seen with a group of highwaymen. As constable, it was his duty to travel to Graystone Manor and question the earl's eldest son. He demanded to know Laney's whereabouts during the past night. I immediately stepped forward and lied to one and all that Laney and I had been in each other's company during that time, claiming we'd both found sleep to elude us and had happened upon each other in the garden where we'd shared conversation and the reading aloud of poetry. My father, of course, was thunderstruck and feared for my reputation, but in the end nothing came of it, and the cloud of suspicion around Laney cleared. He later swore he would be forever in my debt for coming to his aid. He told me that should I ever find need of him or his help, he would travel to the ends of the earth to do my bidding. I now hope he hasn't forgotten his promise."

"Was he," Peach asked, "in the company of highwaymen that night?"

Meredith stilled. "I believe so, yes . . . but he was not with them when they robbed the coach in question, of that I am certain."

Peach grew thoughtful. "No doubt it was his twin, Larkin, who was at the scene of the crime," she hazarded. "The two of them were often mistaken one for the other in the past, and everyone knows Larkin always did find trouble—or else caused it."

Meredith looked at Peach. "Whoever it was, it wasn't Laney who robbed the coach. He has forever been trustworthy and true, and every inch a gentleman. I'd give him my own life."

"Dearest Merry," said Peach, "by asking the man to marry you, you have done just that."

Meredith took a long sip of her coffee, staring at nothing in particular. "Yes, I have, haven't I?"

"I should tell you now, Merry, there are bets being laid at White's," Peach said.

Meredith returned her gaze to her friend, a puzzled expression in her amber eyes. "As there always are. Why ever should that concern me?"

"Because this particular wager begins and will end with you, my dear."

Meredith set down her cup. "You've quite befuddled me now."

"I doubt that you could ever be befuddled," Peach said, eyeing her friend. "The gaming gentleman are betting on who will or will not see you to the altar, my dear. Not only are you known as 'One of Those Darlington Cousins,' but you have now firmly entrenched yourself in the minds of the many unmarried gentlemen as 'The Marriageable Miss Meredith.' "

Meredith rolled her eyes. "Truly, Peach, the gentleman of White's and many other clubs would just as quickly bet on which raindrop might trickle down to reach the windowpane first! I prefer not to hear about their latest wagers, even if the same do indeed refer to me."

"Just thought I'd mention it, my dear." Peach nodded to the note Meredith held. "You don't suppose Lord Graystone has caught the latest gambling fever, do you? Might there be a chance his lordship has placed a few bets in his own interest?"

"No," said Meredith with assurance. "Laney is my friend. A confidante."

"Very well then," said Peach. "Let us assume he isn't wagering to be the one to marry you. Let us even assume he hasn't any interest in your vast inheritance, and that he is sincere about the promise he made to you those many years ago. That leaves only one thing to worry about, my dear Merry."

"Which is?"

"Do you truly think his lordship will understand your involvement in the Midnight Society? After all, if he is the man you will soon marry, he'd best be understanding of *that*."

"I don't know for certain," Meredith honestly replied.

"I am obviously hoping that will be the way of it. After all, our society is very dear to me. I am not about to cease my involvement with it."

"I am glad to hear you say as much, Meredith, for I believe we are very near to a breakthrough."

Meredith lifted one brow, her thoughts veering away from her own worries. "Oh?"

"Yes. I think one of the women we seek to help is very much prepared to allow us into her life." Peach's voice dropped a note as she leaned forward. "I've had word this morning that a woman called Suzanne is hoping to free herself from the horrors of Madame Blue's. Rumour is she is unwilling to raise her young son in such a place, and she very much wants to cut all ties with the poisonous Madame Blue. It is my belief that if your Stubbins will once again venture into the lawless, dockside area to deliver yet another note, she might be persuaded to flee soon. We can again offer Suzanne and her young son a safe place to go. I believe the woman is only faltering because she fears what might become of herself and her child should the funds of our society suddenly be cut off."

"But they shan't be cut off!" said Meredith.

"No," agreed Peach. "Not anytime soon, that is. But we must be realistic, Meredith. Our secretive society cannot continue as it has been. Our many members have only the pin money their husbands allot to them. It takes a great deal of blunt to house, clothe, and feed the many women we have promised to aid. I fear our coffers are running dry. I'd give more myself, but I've already dug deep into my pockets."

"I could give a great deal more if not for my father's

will," said Meredith passionately. "If only I had complete control of my capital . . ."

"But you don't," Peach reminded her gently.

"If my plans go as hoped—"

"Dear Merry," Peach interrupted. "If your plans are put into motion, you will soon be wed and for any woman that means her fortune will be ruled by her husband."

"Yes, but that husband will be Laney and *he* will certainly understand my penchant to help the downtrodden, or at least I am hoping he will understand," said Meredith.

Peach wasn't convinced. "Lord Graystone comes from a family that has had little pity for the less fortunate. Other than Laney's brother, Larkin, his family made a habit of turning their collective backs on the plight of the poor. The second Earl of Graystone was a powerful figure in Parliament. He did not attain such power by being kind and understanding."

"But Laney has a good heart. A pure heart," insisted Meredith.

"Do not forget he also has the blood of his father in him." Peach shook her head. "I'm sorry, Meredith, but I still do not believe Laney should be your choice. He is too much given to carrying on the cold Graystone legacy. He might have good intentions, but he is still a Graystone at heart. As for his twin, Larkin, I would suggest *he* might be a better choice when it comes to such a thing as aiding the less fortunate, but that one was far too moody and brooding. He was always a loose cannon. No, Merry, I fear the Graystone family is not the choice for you."

Meredith sat back, taking a long drink of coffee that

had gone cold. Could Peach be correct? Could Laney be too much like his heartless father? Or worse, could Laney have truly taken on the shades of his brother, Larkin, who had long been known to be an enigma of a man?

She looked down at the gift he'd sent her, and the note, and wondered again if she'd made a grave error in choosing Laney as her intended. He'd changed, obviously. The question was, had he changed for good or worse?

"I must hold true to my belief that Laney will understand my involvement with our secretive society," Meredith finally said. "I cannot believe he's grown to be as heartless as his father was, or even as volatile as his twin is purported as having been at one time. I must hold only optimistic thoughts, Peach."

"And why is that?"

"Because," murmured Meredith, "I cannot imagine myself being married to anyone but him."

Peach set down her own coffee cup, obviously not pleased and just as obviously not wanting to upset her friend. "Very well," said she.

Meredith looked up, surprised. "You are agreeing with me, Peach?"

"No, dear Merry, not that. But I shall indulge you. You are my friend, afterall. My dearest, sweetest friend. As such, I can do no less."

"Thank you, Peach."

The two of them soon set their minds to the task of penning a missive to Suzanne, a woman who had lived a lifetime of sin and seemed ready enough to leave that same life behind her. Peach and Meredith, and all of the Midnight Society wished to give her that very opportunity. Since the inception of their group, they'd managed to aid a number of women and their children.

Stubbins soon set out on his way, heading into the more lawless parts of Town in search of a female named Suzanne, and bearing a letter that offered the woman and her young son a way out of the life of sin Suzanne led.

Peach later took her leave, and Meredith was left alone in the still-sunny parlor, with a bit of cold toast, and a brief note from Laney that bore neither his trademark signature nor his penchant for writing longer missives.

Meredith wondered again if she'd made a mistake in choosing this "new" Laney as her intended bridegroom.

Even so, she could not deny the flutter of excitement his note had brought to her. Couldn't deny the fact she hoped to see him again even though he was not entirely the person she remembered and was very much an enigma to her.

She saw Laney later that day, on the Pall Mall, as she and Julianne were buying some lemon ice. He looked very handsome in his dark blue coat and fawn-colored inexpressibles, polished boots, and tall top hat. He approached her just as Julianne was engaged in conversation with others near them, and Meredith felt once again as though there were only the two of them in the world. There wasn't much time to converse, but in those few stolen moments he paid for their lemon ice, tipped his hat, and told her he thought she looked a vision.

Meredith thanked him for the gift of Byron's words.

He told her it was something he'd wished to do, and that the pleasure was entirely his.

The crowd about them grew, and they soon found themselves apart again.

She saw him in the park, while she and Julianne, twirling their parasols, took a walk.

He rode on horseback. He was alone. He merely tipped his hat in her direction, smiling that handsome, wondrous smile of his—a smile that was so like and yet so very unlike the Laney she remembered.

And still later, when Meredith ensured that Julianne enjoyed a night of the theater, Meredith espied Lord Graystone across the floodlights of the stage, sitting in his box. He nodded her way. At the intermission, he was there, in the long hallway, and again he smiled. She smiled, too, feeling a private joy that they continually managed to see each other.

By the time the intermission had ended, and Julianne was once again moving toward the box she and Meredith shared, he was suddenly beside her.

They had only a few moments to talk about the play, about how enjoyable it was. Too soon, though, people were jostling about, hurrying back to their seats, and Meredith found herself apart from him again—but not before she mentioned Lady Darcy's card-party set for the next night.

He mentioned he might attend.

Eight

Lady Darcy's card-party was not at all a tiny, informal gathering, but rather a great to-do. The small ballroom of the townhouse had been set with numerous tables for four, as whist was to be the central function, but even more tables had been set up for diners in the adjoining supper-room. A veritable feast had been laid out on buffet tables in that same room, and the many arrangements of flowers filled the room with an explosion of color and nearly threatened to take over every table. The same held true of the ballroom.

Though the time of year made it impossible to invite the cream of the *ton,* the Capital was not totally empty of good Society. There resided a number of fashionable persons in Town as those who had summered outside of the City were beginning to return.

Meredith, joined by Julianne and Lady Beveridge, raised her eyebrows as she tallied up the number of eligible gentleman present; they outnumbered the ladies.

It was apparent Peach knew exactly what thought was in Meredith's mind. "Had this been a formal dinner-party, Merry, Lady Darcy would have paid careful attention to see that the numbers turned out even," Peach whispered. "But she's hoping to see Julianne catches a husband, and that *you,* my dear, might find some fine gentleman to turn your eye to marriage this night as well."

"Me?" said Meredith. "I cannot imagine why Lady Darcy would care a whit as to whether I make it to the altar or not."

Peach smiled knowingly. "Dear Merry, do you remember that your father was an inveterate charmer. Lady Darcy was one of his first loves. Are you shocked? No, I hadn't thought you would be. They never married, of course, since Althea felt she must make her parents proud by marrying a man of blue blood, but she and Manny never forgot each other either. Lady Darcy has a particular interest in you since you are Manny's daughter, and she is only trying to help propel you to the altar because she adored Manny and would like to see that his only child has a suitable match."

"But I've no need of a matchmaker, Peach. You know that."

"Indeed I do. I never once considered you might not yet find yourself the perfect partner in life."

They paused in their conversation as their hostess came forward to greet them. Lady Darcy, a tall, stately woman immediately smiled at sight of Meredith and Julianne. Her bright smile warmed her watery-gray eyes and made Meredith think of the younger Althea her father had loved at one time. She'd immediately liked Lady Darcy when that one had welcomed her into the exclusive Minerva's—and the even more exclusive Midnight Society—and now she was glad to know that her father and the woman had at one time been close.

Lady Darcy gave Meredith a quick hug. "You are stunning as usual, Meredith. I am so glad you came this evening."

"As am I," Meredith replied. "Your stay in Bath must have agreed with you, Lady Darcy, for you are looking very well."

"Bath was a pleasure, as always, but I found myself looking forward to returning to Town and again seeing my friends at Minerva's—and also continuing our ventures in the Midnight Society." She turned to give Peach a kiss on the cheek and a squeeze of her gloved hands. "We must all get together soon. I am very eager to hear if any headway has been made in our latest endeavor for the Midnight Society."

Peach nodded knowingly. "There is some news to be had."

"Good news, in fact," Meredith added. "Our newest mission is promising to be a success. In fact, come tomorrow, we should know the total outcome of it."

"Ah," replied Lady Darcy, and her eyes lit with pleasure. "Leave it to you and Peach to do our Society proud. You must tell all, but not here. We shall get together to discuss all of this soon." She turned to Julianne, the glow not leaving her gaze. "My sweet Julianne, how fetching you look this night! I daresay that particular shade of blue brings out the best in you."

"Thank you," Julianne murmured. "The color was Meredith's choice, and just the other day we chose another bolt of cloth. Gold, I believe, though I cannot quite recall as I had just found the most wonderful collection of poetry at a bookfair in Town."

Lady Darcy hid a frown at mention of poetry. Though she, too, enjoyed reading she was of the mind that Julianne had had her nose stuck in a book for too many years. The ladies at Minerva's had decided to find Julianne a good husband, yet to do so would mean guid-

ing Julianne gently away from her penchant to hide behind a book and to create verse from sunup to sundown.

"Yes, well, you can tell me all about the poetry another
time," replied Lady Darcy. "Tonight, my sweet, I hope
to see you reacquainted with some of the fine gentlemen
you met during the last Season. Now mind you, given
the time of year it is deuced difficult to come up with
a sufficient number for any kind of gathering, but I am
rather pleased with tonight's turnout."

She threaded her arm through Julianne's, leading her
friends toward the ballroom. "Over there is Lord Linsey,
you remember him, do you not, Julianne? I believe he
claimed your first waltz a time ago. He has matured since
then, I swear. Has recently come into his title and is not
so given to avoiding parson's mousetrap. And over there
is Lord Avery. He has just returned to Town from his
country estate. He is not as plump in the pocket as Lord
Linsey, but remains quite a catch nonetheless. And
Meredith, do you see that handsome young man standing
engaged in conversation with Lord Linsey?"

Meredith took note. "Yes, I do, but I can't say as I
know of him, Lady Darcy."

"I am not surprised. He has been gone from Town for
some time. He is Lord Reginald Thornwood and is just
returned from the Continent. He keeps to himself, usu-
ally, so his having accepted my invitation is a pleasant
surprise. I should think you would like to meet him,
Meredith, for I've the feeling the two of you would get
along famously." With that, Lady Darcy picked up pace
and heralded the timid Julianne fully into the ballroom.

Meredith paused a moment, halting Peach alongside
her. She'd heard the note of intent in Lady Darcy's voice

when that one had suggested Meredith get to know the dashing and golden-haired Lord Thornwood.

"Peach, tell me true," Meredith whispered. "What is all this nonsense about finding a perfect parti for me? I do not think Lady Darcy returned early from Bath only because she intended to aid me in a search for a husband."

Peach tut-tutted. "Of course she didn't return for that sole purpose. As you know, she is very much involved with the Midnight Society, and is eager to resume her activity with our group. But I will admit she returned for other reasons as well. Both Althea and I wish to see Julianne married for the simple fact that if she doesn't soon marry, her parents will force her into the countryside to become a spinster for all time. As for our wish to see you marry as well, we only want you to be happy . . . and honoring your father's will seems to be your most pressing desire. Since you are set on being married before your next natal day, my dear Merry, Althea and I decided we would help both Julianne and you in finding suitable matches."

"I appreciate the interest, but I am quite capable of finding my own bridegroom," Meredith reminded her friend.

"Yes, yes, of course you *think* you are. But you haven't much time left, and where there is haste there is the possibility of making a mistake. We wouldn't want you to trip into a union with just *any* gentleman."

Meredith eyed her friend critically. "You are referring to Lord Graystone, I take it."

"I saw how you looked after your moments in Hyde Park with him and then later when you read his note. You have been dreamy-eyed as any schoolgirl experiencing her first crush of love. It bodes ill for any woman to be so swept off her feet by a man who is . . . is, oh, never mind."

"Is what? Say what is on your mind, Peach. And do hurry, as we cannot linger at the threshold of the ball-room much longer without notice."

"You, dear Merry, could never linger anywhere without notice," said Peach, and here she smiled.

At that instant, Meredith knew she would forgive her elderly friend anything.

Peach squeezed her friend's hand, asking for under-standing with that gesture. Whispered she, "Lord Graystone is not the one for you—at least not as he is now. He is too far changed from the gentle soul you claim he was during that summer at Graystone Manor. Now please, let us not spoil this card-party even before it has begun. Lady Darcy intends only to help you and Julianne find a match. There is nothing so terrible about that, is there? Perhaps you shall meet someone this evening who will move you in a way Lord Graystone cannot."

So saying, Peach moved forward and Meredith was forced to do the same. Meredith did not mind that Lady Darcy thought to help Julianne, what she *did* mind was that somehow her own unmarried state had become one of Lady Darcy's missions. She had no need of a Cupid in her midst. All she needed was a private hour with Laney; time enough for the two of them to talk as they had once talked and to fall into the close friendship they'd once known.

But as Meredith and Peach moved inside the ballroom, Meredith had to silently agree with her friend on one point: Laney was not at all as he had been in the past.

No, he was something more. Something all together totally different than the young man she remembered.

* * *

The evening passed pleasantly enough and Meredith later found herself involved in a game of whist with Julianne, the Honorable Jonathan Wheaton and Lord Thornwood. Mr. Wheaton was the third or fourth son of a viscount and so had not been pressed upon the timid Julianne by Lady Darcy, but the young man had flocked to the girl's side nonetheless. He proved to be a boastful sort who seemed to think everyone wished to hear any and all of his less-than-interesting stories.

Julianne, her mind on the game, did not pay him much heed, which only served to make Mr. Wheaton's tongue flap at an even more alarming pace. Meredith might have found herself with a headache if not for the pleasant company of Lord Thornwood.

She'd at first thought him far too handsome for his own good. He looked like a veritable god in his dark-blue coat, superbly cut, and cream breeches. His hair was the color of wheat burned golden by a bright sun, and his eyes were a deep shade of blue. He easily manipulated Mr. Wheaton into a more tolerable conversation; namely, anything that had not to do with Wheaton himself.

Meredith was glad of Lord Thornwood's company. She sensed he knew this to be true. She reminded herself not to smile overly much at him, no matter how grateful she was to have him in on this hand of whist for she did not wish to falsely invite his suit. But try as she might, she couldn't help but feel her lips twitch as Lord Thornwood cleverly bested Wheaton at every verbal turn.

As they ended yet another game and Mr. Wheaton nearly tripped over his own ungainly legs in fetching a glass of punch for Julianne, Lord Thornwood sat back and let out an exaggerated sigh.

"Gadzooks, zounds, and i'faith," exclaimed he, "but I did not think the man would ever cease telling us about himself! I dare swear we now know what the man is about every moment of every day."

"Not to mention why he chose to fashion himself all in yellow this evening," added Meredith, unable to help herself.

Thornwood grinned. "Ah, but it brings young Wheaton staggering good luck to wear yellow, does it not?"

They shared a bit of laughter then, and even Julianne joined in their merriment at poor Wheaton's expense.

"Do you think he intends to join us for another game of whist?" Julianne asked shyly, and then on a rather bold note, added, "I fear he isn't a very good player. He is too busy seeing whether or not anyone is looking his way."

Lord Thornwood laughed all the more at that. "How right you are, Miss Beveridge. Mr. Wheaton would do better to pay closer attention to his cards than the commotion of the room. You, however, are very good at whist."

Julianne blushed prettily, lowering her lashes. "I enjoy the challenge of a good game . . . almost as much as I enjoy poetry."

"You like poetry?" asked Thornwood.

Julianne nodded, and then blushed again.

Meredith knew instantly the young woman was interested in the man. She looked at Thornwood. "Miss Beveridge is fond of creating her own verse," she said, hoping her friend would not be upset by her telling of Julianne's private passion. "Indeed, she is very good at turning a phrase."

Lord Thornwood's blue eyes deepened in color as he glanced first at Meredith and then at Julianne. "Really? I should like to hear some of your verses, Miss Beveridge."

Meredith feared she'd gone too far then; Julianne had never recited her poems to anyone other than herself and Peach.

Julianne, however, lifted her face to Lord Thornwood and gave him the most wonderful smile Meredith had ever seen from her.

"I would like that very much," Julianne replied, surprising Meredith with such words.

Mr. Wheaton returned then, bearing not only a glass of punch for Julianne, but one for Meredith as well. At his insistence, they all settled in for yet another game of whist, and for more stories of Wheaton's dull existence. As he began retelling his woes of having broken a heel just as he'd intended to head for Lady Darcy's this night, even Julianne hid a smile.

Meredith decided that being paired with Lord Thornton and Mr. Wheaton this night had been good for Julianne. She was glad they'd come, but disappointed Laney was not in attendance.

Suddenly, she spied a latecomer to the gathering. It was well after ten, and yet the man entered the room as though he was not unfashionably late and risking the ire of their hostess.

The man was none other than the third Earl of Graystone.

"Is that not the gentleman you were speaking with at the library the other day?" whispered the innocent Julianne.

Meredith felt her heart thump wildly at the sight of

Laney. He was dressed wholly in black, with nothing more than his snowy linens, rich coppery hair, and vivid green eyes adding dashing color to his attire. His gaze swept the room once, and then after focusing on her companions held on Meredith. She thought she saw him frown.

"He is the one," Meredith whispered in reply to Julianne's question, and was for once glad that Mr. Wheaton was chatting nonstop as usual.

Lord Thornwood, however, had clearly blotted out young Wheaton's drone and heard Julianne's and Meredith's exchange.

"You and Lord Graystone are acquainted, Miss Darlington?" he asked.

Meredith forcefully pulled her gaze from the sight of Laney who, pointedly ignoring her, paid his respects to Lady Darcy and then moved away to converse with a group of his peers in the far corner. The fact that Laney had seen her seated with her friends and had just as quickly pulled his gaze away, unsettled her greatly.

"Excuse me?" she said to Lord Thornwood.

He was eyeing her closely. "Lord Graystone. You know him?"

"Yes," she answered absently. "His father and mine were friends at one time. Laney . . . er, Lord Graystone and I met briefly one summer long ago."

"I see," Lord Thornwood replied, and if he noticed her use of Graystone's Christian name, he made no show of it.

Lady Darcy chose that moment to interrupt. She bent down toward Julianne and said there was someone she wished for her to meet. The next thing Meredith knew, Julianne had had been forced to abandon their half-finished game of whist and was soon following in Lady Darcy's wake. A frowning Mr. Wheaton chose that moment to excuse himself as well, and Meredith and Lord Thornwood were left to themselves.

Lord Thornwood pushed his cards to the middle of the table. "I find I grow weary of cards, Miss Darlington. What say you to a stroll about the room, and perhaps a walk in Lady Darcy's garden? I hear her gardener is the best in Town and that he has been busy during her weeks away. Shall we pay him homage and view his handiwork in the moonlight?"

Meredith would never have agreed to such a thing if her thoughts weren't on Laney and how he'd ignored her upon his arrival. She was of no mind to stay in the room and wonder when—or even if—he would bother to say hello.

She turned her face to Lord Thornwood. "I think a turn about the room, and perhaps even a bit of fresh air, would do me good, my lord."

He was to his feet in an instant and offering her his arm. Together, the two of them headed around the parameter of the room.

Larkin glowered as he watched Meredith being led ever closer to the terrace doors, and on the arm of the doubtable Lord Thornwood, no less. The man was jaded, a heartless being, and not above underhanded dealings. He was, in a word, detestable.

Larkin wondered what the marriageable Miss Meredith was doing in allowing Thornwood to lead her toward the darkness of the garden. Perhaps she'd decided that Laney, or rather he, himself, wasn't what she'd wished for in a bridegroom. Or perhaps—and here, Larkin's features darkened even more—Meredith and Thornwood were co-horts in some grand scheme.

It was no secret to Larkin that Thornwood's father had suffered a lowering setdown due to the fact he and Larkin's father had come to blows over the same woman in their youth. That lady had been Amabel, Larkin's and Laney's mother. It was a further disgrace to Thornwood's family that his father had run into dun territory and soon owed a great deal of money to his age-old enemy since Amabel had beseeched her husband to take pity on the man and forward him some much-needed funds. The loans continued until the elder Thornwood soon owed staggering sums to the second Earl of Graystone. Sums he could ill afford to repay. He was nearly penniless from his gambling sickness and his penchant to keep a mistress in every fashionable city of Europe.

Unable to cope with the disgrace he'd brought upon his family, the man had shot himself in the head, leaving behind a grieving family, a mountain of debt, and a letter that blamed Graystone for all of his woes.

Now, even though both men were dead and buried, the animosity between the Graystones and the Thornwoods was not by far forgotten. Lord Reginald Thornwood held a singular distaste for anything that was even slightly blemished by the Graystone name.

Larkin, Laney, and Reginald had gone to the same schools, and while Laney had chosen to try and make a friend of Reggie (as Laney had called him in their salad days) Larkin could never suffer the fool. He and Reginald had blackened each other's eyes too many times to count. When they'd reached manhood, their youthful fisticuffs had taken a decidedly dangerous turn. Always, they'd tried to undermine each other whenever they'd come into

contact. They were the worst kind of enemies; the seed
of animosity between them had been sown during their
stormy youths and then allowed to grow through the
years of young adulthood. . . .

Larkin now leaned against the mantelpiece in Lady
Darcy's over-decorated ballroom, and found himself ru-
minating. He did not like that Meredith might soon be
alone with Thornwood. He didn't like it at all.

He would have gone after them, but Lady Darcy took
that moment to approach him.

"Lord Graystone," said she, "may I introduce to you
Miss Julianne Beveridge? I do not believe you were in
Town last Season when Miss Beveridge had her come-
out."

One of many, thought Larkin to himself as he bowed
over the young woman's hand. He knew enough of the
ton, via Drake, to know that poor Miss Julianne
Beveridge had been foisted into Society on more than
one occasion. He wondered why her disinterested parents
did not just allow the woman her own head to do as she
pleased which was obviously not to suffer through yet
another embarrassing come-out. Surely, one was enough
for any female to endure.

"It is a pleasure to meet you, Miss Beveridge," he
said, and meant it. She seemed pleasant, and what he
had heard about her from Drake was enough to make
him warm to her immediately. Drake had said she'd liked
poetry and was given to hiding herself away from polite
company while she penned numerous verses a day.

She reminded Larkin of Laney in that respect. Laney,

PRESENTING AN IRRESISTIBLE OFFERING ON YOUR KIND OF ROMANCE.

Receive 4 Zebra Regency Romance Novels (A $16.47 value)

Free

Journey back to the romantic Regent Era with the world's finest romance authors. Zebra Regency Romance novels place you amongst the English *ton* of a distant past with witty dialogue, and stories of courtship so real, you feel that you're living them!

Experience it all through 4 FREE Zebra Regency Romance novels...yours just for the asking. When you join *the only book club dedicated to Regency Romance readers,* additional Regency Romances can be yours to preview FREE each month, with no obligation to buy anything, ever.

Regency Subscribers Get First-Class Savings.

After your initial package of 4 FREE books, you'll begin to receive monthly shipments of new Zebra Regency titles. These all new novels will be delivered direct to your home as soon as they are published...sometimes even before the bookstores get them! Each monthly shipment of 4 books will be yours to examine for 10 days. Then, if you decide to keep the books, you'll pay the pre-ferred subscriber's price of just $3.30 per title. That's $13.20 for all 4 books...a savings of over $3 off the publisher's price! What's more, $13.20 is your <u>total</u> price...there's no additional charge for shipping and handling.

No Minimum Purchase, a Generous Return Privilege, and FREE Home Delivery!

We're so sure that you'll appreciate the money-saving convenience of home delivery that we <u>guarantee</u> your complete satisfaction. You may return any shipment...for any reason...within 10 days and pay nothing that month. And if you want us to stop sending books, just say the word. There is no mini-mum number of books you must buy.

COMPLETE AND RETURN THE ORDER CARD TO RECEIVE THIS $16.47 VALUE. **ABSOLUTELY FREE.**

(If the certificate is missing below, write to: Zebra Home Subscription Service, Inc., 120 Brighton Road, P.O. Box 5214, Clifton, New Jersey 07015-5214

4 FREE BOOKS

Yes! Please send me 4 Zebra Regency Romances without cost or obligation. I understand that each month thereafter I will be able to preview 4 new Regency Romances FREE for 10 days. Then, if I should decide to keep them, I will pay the money-saving preferred subscriber's price of just $13.20 for all 4...that's a savings of over $3 off the publisher's price with no additional charge for shipping and handling. I may return any shipment within 10 days and owe nothing, and I may cancel this subscription at any time. My 4 FREE books will be mine to keep in any case.

Name _____

Address _____ Apt. _____

City _____ State _____ Zip _____

Telephone ( ) _____

Signature _____

(If under 18, parent or guardian must sign.)

RF0895

Terms and prices subject to change. Orders subject to acceptance by Zebra Home Subscription Service, Inc.

ZEBRA HOME SUBSCRIPTION SERVICE, INC.

120 BRIGHTON ROAD

P.O. BOX 5214

CLIFTON, NEW JERSEY 07015-5214

AFFIX
STAMP
HERE

too, had been quiet and much given to burrowing himself in a library.

Larkin pleased Lady Darcy, no doubt, when he guided Miss Beveridge to the buffet table, procured for her a plate with a few sweets, and then encouraged her to speak of writers and writing.

Lady Darcy left the two of them alone, and Larkin listened as Miss Beveridge spoke of the works of Wordsworth and Coleridge and of Southey.

Larkin decided then that his brother would doubtless find a kindred soul in one Miss Julianne Beveridge.

Larkin moved his gaze beyond Miss Beveridge, seeing that Meredith and Thornwood had completed their circle of the room and were now heading out into the garden. It was a designated area, lit with a few lamps, and so for Meredith to stroll with Thornwood there would not mar her reputation. Many other couples had taken air together, and no one had looked askance.

Larkin, though, felt something harden inside of him. He quickly saw to it Miss Beveridge was once again beneath the watchful eyes of Lady Darcy, excused himself from their company, and then headed for the terrace doors. He couldn't help but wonder if perhaps Thornwood was the murderous enemy he sought . . . and if, perhaps, Meredith was the man's cohort.

Lady Darcy's townhouse garden was a indeed a delight. There was a flagstone walkway, lit by hanging lanterns, and even though there hadn't been a great deal of space for the layout, the gardener had created a veritable Eden. The scent of blooming flowers and greenery filled the cool, evening air.

Meredith would have rather been enjoying the moon-and-lantern-lit night with Laney. What silliness, though. Laney had looked at her as though he'd like to slice her head from her neck when he'd entered Lady Darcy's and seen her caught up in a game of whist with her partners. Now why was that? she wondered. Whatever had she done to make him so angry?

"You are suddenly quiet," said Lord Thornwood, maneuvering Meredith around a bend in the walkway.

They were threading further and further from the house and closer to the mews that stood beyond the high garden wall. Meredith noted that the hanging lanterns did not reach this far back. She came to a standstill.

"Am I? I do not mean to be."

He smiled. She noted that his teeth were very bright and white in the dark night. "If I may be so bold, Miss Darlington, I do believe your thoughts are on Lord Graystone this night. I noted your reaction to his arrival. You were surprised and yet pleased to see he'd decided to grace Lady Darcy with his presence."

Meredith stiffened. Lord Thornwood had noticed all of *that?* She must do better to hide her emotions. "I—I was merely surprised to see him, my lord. It is rumored, after all, that Lord Graystone is not one to be present at many social gatherings."

"No," he agreed. "He isn't. Not lately, anyway. There was a time, however, when Lord Graystone was given to attending as many gatherings as his schedule allowed."

"My lord?" she replied, feeling he'd meant to say more.

"I mean only that Lord Graystone of late is acting rather peculiar. You see, he and I were the best of friends during our university days. We'd lost contact in the years following, but just before this past Season the two of us finally managed to get reacquainted in the weeks prior to my heading for the Continent. I must say, though, he's changed in just the short span of time since I saw him last. There is something about him that isn't quite the same . . . and the fact that he arrived shockingly late at this card-party only confirms this notion."

"He did arrive late," remarked Meredith, and wondered why he'd even come at all. He obviously did not intend to speak with her. The realization smarted, causing Meredith to frown. Why he'd nearly glared at her with contempt upon entering Lady Darcy's home was also a puzzle to her.

But then again, Meredith thought to herself, the reason might simply be he'd been off-set that she was deep in a card game and unreachable. To come forward and claim her time would have been to draw all eyes to the two of them and of course Laney would not do such a thing. He was far too private a person for public displays.

Meredith suddenly knew an urgent need to be back inside so that she could make herself readily available for Laney should he want to approach her. She returned her thoughts to Lord Thornwood.

"I—I do believe I am feeling a bit chilly," she said. "If you don't mind, my lord, I would like to go back inside."

Lord Thornwood, eyeing her closely, nodded. "Of course," he murmured solicitously.

They headed back the way they'd come.

Meredith decided then Lord Thornwood was not a man without character. If he'd thought to take advantage of their private walk in the garden, he hadn't done so. Instead, he proved to be quite pleasant. When he began to talk of Julianne and his hope of seeing her again, Meredith was even more pleased.

"I should think another meeting betwixt the two of you could be arranged," offered Meredith.

"Oh?" he said, and his eyes took on a lively shine.

"She is to attend a balloon ascension later this week on the outskirts of Town. If you were to attend as well, I shouldn't see any reason why the two of you would not have an opportunity to speak with each other."

"And will you be present as well, Miss Darlington?"

Meredith thought he'd hoped she would be present only so that she could steer he and Julianne in the same direction.

She nodded. "Of course. The outing was my idea."

Lord Thornwood smiled. "I am not surprised." He took the liberty of plucking a late bloom from Lady Darcy's garden. "Dare I hope since Miss Beveridge enjoys poetry, she will also find pleasure in a flower chosen just for her?"

Meredith, who knew Julianne had been instantly smitten with the man, nodded. She thought Lord Thornwood to be a most serious and pleasant suitor for her friend.

"I can only pray you are correct," he replied.

Meredith was feeling light of heart as Lord Thornwood guided her inside. But it was then that her light mood came to a crushing end for in the doorway stood the indomitable figure of Lane Markham Graystone. It gave Meredith no hope at all to know he was staring at her with what could only be described as outright anger.

Now what the devil could she have done to cause his ire? she wondered.

Unfortunately, she was about to find out.

Nine

"My lord," Meredith whispered.

"Good evening, Miss Darlington. Lord Thornwood." He nodded woodenly at the two of them.

Though Lord Thornwood returned Graystone's nod, Meredith could see the tenseness in him. She sensed a rising storm between the two men and hastened to get them out of each other's reach. "We were just heading back inside, my lord," she said to Laney.

"For another game of whist, I take it," he said, and he did not sound in the least bit pleased. His gaze flicked over Lord Thornwood then. "You'll forgive us, I trust, Thornwood, but Miss Darlington has previously promised to allow me the pleasure of showing her Lady Darcy's garden."

"Pity that," said Lord Thornwood not at all thwarted by Graystone's words or even the intensity with which the man spoke them, "but you are a moment too late. I have just shown Miss Darlington the gardens."

A muscle twitched ominously along Graystone's jawline. "I doubt," said he, "that Miss Darlington would be pleased to go home without having viewed the particular flower I wished to show her this night. It is a rare breed. Quite exquisite."

"I believe Miss Darlington and I have viewed all of the

garden's delights," Lord Thornwood said to Graystone, his tone almost taunting.

"Even so, I cannot believe you managed to call this particular bloom to her attention," said Graystone dryly. "It is one that must be searched for." He abruptly turned his gaze to Meredith's. "Shall we?" he asked.

Meredith felt her eyes blaze as she met his arrogant features. What deliberate game did he fashion to play? But she knew Lord Thornwood watched their every move. To be truthful and say she'd never promised such a thing would have been to make an issue of it.

Before she could even think clearly, she heard herself say, "Yes. Of course. How—how remiss of me. Lord Thornwood?" she said, giving him a smile she hoped did not appear as tremulous as it felt. "I trust you will not mind if I join Lord Graystone for a moment or two. I shall return even before you notice my absence."

"That," said Lord Thornwood, "is doubtful for I notice your absence already. Please, though, do not allow me to thwart your plans. You will return soon?"

She assured him that she would. Lord Thornwood took his leave, and Meredith and Laney were alone. He held the door open for her as Meredith stepped outside and then he followed.

The night instantly swallowed them. She could not remember the dark being as thick when she'd tread this same path with Lord Thornwood. The scents of the evening, the breeze, the very earth beneath her feet felt startlingly more real.

Silence stretched between them. He did not take her hand in his and place it atop his arm as Lord Thornwood had done, but instead clasped his hands behind his back as they walked slowly toward the far end of the small, enclosed garden.

"You have known Thornwood long?" he finally asked.

She did not want to waste this precious time alone with him in discussing Lord Thornwood, but he seemed determined to do so.

"I have just met him this evening," she answered. "Lady Darcy is most enamored of him, as is Lady Beveridge."

"And you?"

"I find him pleasant enough," she answered truthfully.

"Enough for what, Meredith?"

She glanced up sharply, surprised by the impertinence of his question and disturbed by the deeper, hidden meaning of it. "Is this an inquisition?"

"Of course not. I simply would like to know where Thornwood stands in your estimation."

"As I told you, I have only just met him—"

"Yet you've had time enough to find him 'pleasant.' "

"Something you obviously do not," she replied, noting the stern set of his jaw and the tightness of his handsome mouth.

"You are quite right about that," he said. He took hold of her elbow, guiding her around the slight bend in the walkway, his agitation and anger evident.

"But Lord Thornwood told me the two of you were friends at one time."

He cocked one brow at her. "He told you that, did he?"

"Yes."

"We were friends. Once. People, however, have the cursed habit of changing."

"Oh, yes," she whispered, thinking of the Laney she

once knew, of the friendship they'd shared. "People *do* tend to change."

They were nearing the edges of the garden. Before them stood the tall gate that separated the lush gardens from the mews that stood just beyond it. The only light was that of the moon, and a lone lantern that hung near the gate post.

A cool wind whispered about, fluttering the leaves of the garden and causing the lantern's glow to flicker wildly. Shadows danced. The night that had once seemed so magical when Laney had arrived, suddenly mocked Meredith. She felt cold, chilled to the bone.

Meredith shivered. "There is no special bloom you wished to show me, is there?" she asked.

Meredith thought he might hedge or at least point out some ordinary flower and try, with the right words, to make it appear more than it was. But he didn't.

"No," he answered, his pace not slowing. "There isn't."

She'd known it to be true all along, yet hearing him say so made her heart fall. There was nothing more to say. He'd wanted her away from Lord Thornwood, had wanted to usurp the man in some way. And he had done so. She felt manipulated and used.

"Then I see no reason to continue our walk. I prefer to go back inside."

"I prefer you didn't." His hold on her tightened. His steps quickened.

"Please!" Meredith said to him as he verily dragged her along. "Will you not slow your pace? My gown is not cut for such long strides as yours, and—and truth be told, Laney, I've no idea why you are in such a snit this night!"

"A snit?" he echoed, finally pulling her to a halt beside the high garden wall. "I find you alone with the likes of Thornwood, and you dare ask why I am feeling as I am?"

"But I thought you and Lord Thornwood were friends. At least, you were at one time."

"Do you remember, Meredith, that Thornwood and I were only friends during our salad days at the university."

"No," she said. "I do not remember! And why should I, Laney? The time we shared that summer long ago was taken up not with who was our friend or not, but rather who the two of *us* were. Have you forgotten that?"

Meredith regretted the words as soon as they flew off her tongue. Drat, but she was constantly saying the wrong thing to the man. And her latest words were quite obviously not the words to say.

He appeared rattled. Indeed, he even raked one hand through his coppery hair. "Devil take it!" he muttered.

Meredith broke free of his bruising hold. "Yes," she agreed with him, "the devil should take it, as he should all of your mercurial moods since I met you again!"

Meredith felt tears gathering in her eyes, but was beyond caring that she should cry openly in front of him. He'd hurt her with his less than congenial greeting of her in the park, with his anger earlier this night and even now with his pique that she should stroll in the gardens with Lord Thornwood. Who was *he* to judge *her*? She was her own master, and had been since the day of her dear father's death.

So she'd proposed a marriage of convenience to him, what of it? It did not give him the right to act so harshly with her, especially since he hadn't given her an answer!

And that, blast him, was why she felt tears threatening

her. He'd not given her an answer. He'd not immediately taken her in his arms and soothed all of her fears. He had, instead, said he wished to *ponder* her proposal. Ponder, indeed!

"Blast you, Laney," Meredith suddenly said, through with being patient with him. "I don't know how you can treat me like this! We were such close friends, yet you seem bent on treating me as less than that. How can you?"

Meredith pressed the back of one hand against her mouth, fearing she might heap further insult upon him, and then turned away, crying in spite of her resolve not to.

What a wretched night it had turned out to be.

Larkin saw the shimmer of tears in her beautiful amber eyes just before she pivoted away from him. He suddenly felt a heel. Worse, he felt as though he'd done a terrible injustice to both his brother and to Meredith.

Perhaps Miss Darlington wasn't the supreme actress he'd thought her to be. Dear God in heaven, maybe she *was* Laney's true love.

He cleared his throat, reaching out to touch her slender shoulder. She jerked away from him, of course. "Meredith," he implored her. Still, she did not turn to look at him.

She was playing the role of her life if she wasn't the true friend of Laney's she'd said she was, Larkin thought. He admired her boldness.

Problem was, though, he also admired her spunk. And he liked the way she'd smiled at him in the park. Liked, too, her beautiful face, interesting eyes, and the golden curls that framed her delicate features. He'd also been enchanted by the sight of her in the dusky dark confines of the lending library, with her spectacles slipping down the bridge of her nose, her mind clearly caught up in the tale she'd been reading. And her tears at the moment . . . why, they seemed so deucedly genuine!

Larkin felt his heart do a queer flip-flop at the sounds of her ragged, indrawn breath. He hated that he'd made her cry. She was very good at crying. Made it sound as though she truly meant it. But she was acting, wasn't she? He shouldn't get so sentimental with her.

But he was. Getting sentimental, that is. He saw her shoulders quiver, heard her gasp for yet another breath as she tried to play at being very brave. The moonlight cut a swath across her, haloing her lovely blond hair and casting her light blue gown into a blaze of silver. Her whole body appeared to beam with a soft radiance, and Larkin felt himself warm to her even more.

Laney might have loved her once, Larkin thought. Damme, his brother might *still* love her for all he knew. How could Larkin be so terse with her? How could he continue to treat her as a conspirator if indeed all she claimed was true?

But more to the point . . . how could he handle such a female with anger when all she made him feel was softness? He imagined holding her in his arms, imagined taking the pins from her glorious hair and seeing it fan out on a pillow beneath her head. And he imagined how delectable her body would be beneath his own.

There was no way in all of God's green earth he would allow the likes of the detestable Thornwood to capture the marriageable Miss Darlington's interest. And if Laney had thought once to marry the girl, then who was Larkin to stand in the way?

"Meredith," he heard himself whisper, "will you not turn round so that I can properly propose to you? You said yourself you wished for us to marry. I—I have decided I quite agree with you."

He watched, mesmerized, as she turned slowly to face him.

"Truly, Laney?" she whispered, a few tears still clinging to her beguiling lashes.

Larkin felt as though he were falling into lust and would have to claw his way back out.

"Yes," he said, his voice just a hoarse whisper, ragged with his own raw emotion.

"I—I don't know what to say. I had thought, well, I'd thought you didn't remember me. I thought—"

"Forget all of that," Larkin interrupted, and his voice turned a bit too gruff for his own taste at mention of what she must have thought. "Suffice it to say I have been a perfect ogre. I only hope you will forgive me, and oversee my lack of manners."

"I can. I do."

"Yes. Well." Larkin cleared his throat, wondering what in the blazes he should say now that he'd nearly all but fallen into parson's mousetrap, and in his brother's guise, to boot! "Now that all has been forgiven and forgotten, I s'pose we should set ourselves to the task of hashing out this idea of a marriage betwixt us."

"Of course," Meredith said softly. She folded her hands neatly in front of her, and then looked up at him with wide, amber eyes.

Larkin had to hold himself back from pulling her into a tight embrace. He felt dazed by the sight of her, so enchanting was she in the moon's light. He tried to shake off the lust that suddenly pumped through him. Dear

God, but did she have to appear so enchanting? And there were other things he was feeling at the moment; such as a wondrous kind of elation at the sight of her, and also a deep, deep, interest in the lady's heart.

"We, uh, should plan a time to discuss the . . . the arrangements and so forth," he said, again clearing his throat. Gad, but what a tongue-tied fool he'd suddenly become. He hastened to collect his wits. "What say you to tomorrow? Would that be agreeable?"

Amazingly enough, her pretty brow puckered into a frown. "Tomorrow?"

"Yes, tomorrow," he all but insisted, and then remembering it was Laney she thought she spoke with—had *proposed* to—he added, on a far softer note, "On the morrow in the afternoon is, uh, a very good time for our talk."

"Oh, dear," she murmured, clearly puzzling over whether or not she could manage to ease him into her schedule. "I—I don't know . . ." Her voice trailed off as she considered the offer.

Gadzooks, Larkin thought to himself, using one of Drake's handy phrases. She, after all, had been the one to hound *him*—or rather, Laney—for a marriage proposal. Could she not make room for him in her day? Again, he had the distinct impression she could not at all be the conniving female he sought to uncover. If so, she'd have jumped at any chance to meet with him.

"I—I am afraid I have a previous engagement tomorrow afternoon, Laney."

Then cancel it, b'god, Larkin thought. But he didn't say such a thing. Laney, of course, had forever been a patient sort of fellow.

"You see," she said into the silence that followed, her

brow still puckered, "I have promised to meet with friends and it is *most* imperative I attend this gathering. There is a—a mission my friends and I have embarked upon and I fear I cannot let them down by not attending this gathering. Oh, Laney, I so very much wish to speak with you, and yet tomorrow is not a possibility—"

"Where is this meeting?" he asked, a shade too quickly. "And when?"

"Hanover Square," she answered truthfully. "At noon."

"I am to meet with my solicitor on Holywell Street at that very time. Perhaps you and I could get together at some point later in the day? Say around three? I could meet you near Hanover Square—"

"No," said Meredith quickly, clearly struggling over the idea of telling him more than she wished him to know about her meeting. "I—I would rather meet you near Holywell. I shall find you. Would that be acceptable?"

"If you insist," he replied.

"I do."

He heaved a mental sigh. Being Laney was difficult at times. "Then it is settled."

Meredith all but beamed at him. "I shall see you then."

Larkin nodded, wondering if he'd have the fortitude to get through an afternoon with the lovely Miss Darlington without touching her. He must, though. She thought he was Laney. And Laney, of course, might truly love the woman as much as she obviously loved him.

"Dear Laney," she breathed, her pretty countenance shining in the moonlight, "I promise you I shall be the wife you once told me you desired. I'll not take up a moment more of your time than need be. It shall be a union of trust and friendship. We'll be good for each other, as we'd always intended to be."

"Trust?" he echoed. "Friendship?"

She nodded, still smiling.

Gad, he thought, but she truly intended a marriage in name only.

"Though we were both quite young when we'd decided not to marry for passion but rather for kinship, we knew what we were about, did we not?" she continued. "A true friend is far better than anything. And I am your friend, Laney."

Larkin thought he might choke on his own desire of her. He sternly reminded himself this woman had shared a special something with his brother. He must tread carefully so as not to break any trust she held for Laney.

"How soon do you wish us to be married?" he asked.

"Certainly before my natal day, of course."

"And that is?"

"Within the fortnight," she answered.

It was too soon and yet not soon enough. "Then we must make haste," he heard himself say for he no longer believed she was the spy of his enemy. She was too sincere for that. She was indeed an old and dear friend of Laney's, and as such Larkin knew he must aid her.

However, he was unprepared for the melting smile she bestowed upon him. "Laney," she whispered. "How I adore you. I always knew we would one day be together. I won't fail you. I shall be the perfect wife."

He gave her his best imitation of Laney's smile. And then, as he led her back inside, had the horrid realization that he'd have to marry her in Laney's name if indeed he could not locate his brother by then.

But what troubled Larkin more was the fact he didn't

know whether or not he could leave her untouched as she believed Laney would.

He stopped her just before they entered into the light of the lanterns strung near the door. He gazed long and hard at her lovely face, and knew in that instant there was something he must do.

"What is it, Laney?" she whispered when he neither moved or spoke.

He leaned close to her. "This," Larkin murmured, bending his head near to hers. "I must do this."

He kissed her then, covering her sweet mouth with his own and hoping to once and for all get his wanting of her out of his mind. Surely once he kissed her he would be able to banish the lust for her that he felt . . . surely, since it was Laney she loved and wanted, he would not be able to elicit from her any dreg of keen desire or from himself any shred of true love.

But he'd been a fool to think such a thing for the taste of her was that of honey, and the feel of her mouth against his was soft and pliable and far too delicious. And God help them both, but she responded to his kiss like a flower opening to a warm and beguiling sun.

Larkin's soul suddenly tumbled into a sphere of emotion he'd never before experienced. He felt a tumult of feelings pump through him; excitement, yearning, even contentment. The latter emotion puzzled him most of all.

He pulled back, gazing at Meredith through eyes that saw her in a red haze of passion and an astounding scope of possible happiness.

"I should not have taken that liberty," he said, when in fact he wanted to say he wished to take a thousand more liberties with her. "Forgive me, Meredith."

She looked dazed and dreamy, and just as breathless

as he felt. "There is nothing to forgive, Laney," she murmured, but he could sense she was just as confused by her reaction to his kiss as he had been with his act of kissing her.

"Yes, well, we should get back inside before—" words failed him, and his voice trailed off.

"Before what, Laney?" she asked, both bold and shy all at once.

Gad, thought Larkin. *She is an innocent to what a kiss such as the one we shared can lead to.* And yet, he knew, that should he pursue such another kiss, she would not deny him. She was obviously very much in love with his brother. She trusted Laney. Trusted him with her life, and her virtue.

Larkin silently cursed himself for wanting her. He'd thought that by kissing her he'd prove to himself she wasn't the woman for him.

He'd been wrong.

"Before I do something so reckless as to kiss you again," he finally answered.

She gave him a tremulous smile then, breaking the tense moment. "I have always been reckless, Laney. You alone can attest to that fact. But you are correct; it would indeed be best if we went back inside now."

Larkin collected his wits, then led her inside the house. Meredith immediately found Miss Beveridge and Lady Darcy and was soon involved in conversation with her friends.

Larkin was glad. Who knew what might have happened if she'd remained by his side in the garden.

Lord Thornwood approached then.

"You look a bit unnerved," said Thornwood, sipping a glass of punch.

Larkin lifted one brow, pulling his gaze away from Meredith, and eyeing the man with concealed contempt. "Do I? I can't imagine why."

Lord Reginald Thornwood had the sheer audacity to laugh at that. "Mayhap it is because I've managed to snare the interest of Miss Darlington. Word around Town is that she is determined to see herself married soon. Word also has it she hasn't chosen a bridegroom. I see no reason why I could not be he."

Larkin inwardly fumed. "Stay clear of Miss Darlington, Thornwood."

"Is that a warning . . . or a threat?"

"Make of it what you will. Just stay away from the lady."

Lord Thornwood's mouth thinned into an unholy smile. "You know, Graystone, what they say about you of late is true; you do seem to have taken on the dark shades of your ne'er-do-well twin. In fact, one would be forced to hazard that *you* are *he.*"

Larkin noted the man's veiled sneer, but forced himself not to physically react. To anyone nearby, they appeared to be having a pleasant conversation. "Worried, Reggie?" Larkin asked, giving emphasis to the nickname his brother had often used when conversing with the man.

"Should I be, Laney?" Lord Thornwood countered, just as easily falling into the use of first names.

Larkin gave a grunt of laughter, turning his gaze to the many people milling about. " 'Tis no secret you and my brother shared nothing but contempt for each other. So whether or not you should be worried would depend . . ."

"On what? What the devil are you talking about, Graystone?"

Larkin returned his gaze to the man's countenance. Reginald was clearly growing more nervous by the moment. "Whether or not you've a guilty conscience," Larkin answered.

Lord Thornwood shifted uneasily from one foot to the other. "I fear you've lost me with your cryptic words."

"I doubt that. You always were a wily fox. Do you know, though, that whoever plots to bring pain to my brother does the same to me."

"Are you implying I was somehow involved in Larkin's unfortunate demise?"

"I am not implying anything. I am simply stating a fact." He made a motion to move away, intending to pay his respects to their hostess before he left the party. He stilled a moment, though, adding, "By the way, as far as I am concerned, my brother is very much alive. I've never been one to pay heed to gossip, you know. It would take far more than a nasty rumor to make me believe my brother met a foul end. I should tell you, too, that if indeed my brother has been injured in any way, I will not rest until I avenge the deed. To be quite blunt, I will seek an eye for an eye."

Lord Thornwood stiffened. "Those are appallingly strong words from someone of your gentle disposition, Graystone."

"Ah, but you are mistaken. I am not as gentle as I appear, especially where my brother is concerned—and where Miss Darlington is concerned as well. Do heed my warning; *stay away from the lady.*"

Lord Thornwood's nostrils thinned as he sucked in a breath of air. "And if I do not?"

Larkin didn't bat an eye. "You will regret it," he said simply.

"You mean there will be a challenge, Graystone?"

"If need be."

"How interesting. The choice of weapons would then be mine, would it not?"

"If it came to that, yes."

"I am very skilled with both pistol and sword. The same, *Laney,* cannot be said of you."

Larkin went perfectly still then. He eyed the man with unveiled hatred. "There you err. I am not the young man you once claimed as a friend. Indeed, I am far from that gullible person. I have become very familiar with pistols and swords, and the gray light of dawn is often when I am at my best. Do not tempt me, Thornwood. Do not even dare to try."

So saying, Larkin bowed stiffly, then turned and strode away, feeling Thornwood's heated gaze follow him.

Much later, Julianne leaned back against the squabs of Peach's enclosed carriage. She sighed dreamily. "What an amazing evening," she whispered.

"Indeed," agreed Meredith, who had also settled back for the ride home.

Peach surveyed her two friends. "I trust Lady Darcy's card-party was a success then?"

"Most definitely," enthused Julianne breathlessly.

Meredith, however, was pensively gazing out the window, the gloved fingers of her right hand touching her lips as she remembered Laney's stolen kiss . . . a kiss that had affected her far too greatly.

He'd kissed her the night she'd ridden with him back to the stables during the long-ago summer holiday they'd shared, but the feel of his lips then hadn't moved her as much as this evening. The kiss they'd shared years ago had been brief and chaste; a kiss between newfound friends. It had been a bonding of sorts, a sealing of their trust in each other. Nothing more.

Tonight, however, Laney's kiss had been full of passion and heat and had been totally alarming in its intensity. No simple kiss, this! Not at all. *This* kiss had shaken Meredith all the way to her soul, and had left her shamelessly hungry for more.

Good Lord, she wondered, if that was how he kissed her when there was a room filled with people nearby, how might he kiss her when they were married and alone in their own home?

And he *would* kiss her again and again once they were married, she guessed, for this new Laney was clearly a man of deep passion and deeper need.

Though Meredith had thought they would have a marriage in name only, she suddenly realized how naive she'd been in thinking such a thing. His kiss tonight proved he was no longer the sweet, nonthreatening Laney of her past. He was a man. Wholly. Totally. A man who would claim what was his.

And Meredith would soon be his, in name and all other regards . . .

Her cheeks flamed as she imagined what their wedding night would bring, and all the nights following it. Dear God, what had she gotten herself into? she wondered with alarm.

Peach, seeing Meredith's inner tumult, frowned. "Do not tell me you had a moment alone with Lord Graystone," she whispered to her friend.

Meredith shook herself from her reverie at the sound of her friend's voice. "Very well," she replied. "I shan't."

Peach reached out and took Meredith's left hand in both of hers, squeezing tightly. "You look positively shaken."

Meredith glanced over at her. "I *am* shaken, Peach, and awed and confused and . . . and most likely not making any sense at all! I can't explain it, but Laney is nothing that I remember yet everything I'd been hoping for." She gave a small shake of her head, further words failing her.

"Just beware, dear Merry," whispered Peach. "I should not wish to see you with a broken heart."

"But that is the problem, Peach. He *didn't* break my heart. It would have been far easier, perhaps, if he had. Instead, he has filled it with longings I've never felt before, and he's created in my mind thoughts I've never entertained. He's made me feel strange and new and . . . alive. Yes, that is quite the whole of it; God help me, but I've never felt this alive before. You see, Peach, he—he has proposed to me."

The older woman said nothing for a full minute, and then: "And you accepted."

"Yes, of course I did. It . . . it is what I've been dreaming of and hoping for."

"It is what the *girl* in you dreamed of and hoped for," said Peach softly, "but what about *woman* in you, my dearest Merry?"

"I am not wholly certain, Peach. He—he has proven to be so much more than I'd remembered. The truth is, he frightens me . . . or rather, my reactions to him frighten me."

"When do you plan on seeing him again?" Peach asked, clearly realizing that Meredith and his lordship had yet to truly discuss in detail their coming marriage.

"Tomorrow," Meredith admitted. "I am to meet him on Holywell Street, after our meeting with Lady Darcy and after his own with his solicitor."

"And?" the intuitive Peach pressed.

"He said we would . . . talk."

"From the look on your face, Meredith, the last thing the two of you want to do is talk." She sighed, settling back, still holding Meredith's hand. "Just do be careful, my dear. Promise me you will proceed with caution and not be hastened into anything just because of your father's will. I would so hate for your precious heart to be crushed by the inveterate charmer Lord Graystone has obviously become. If he unsettles you then pray, do not proceed with your plan. Do you remember there are other gentleman for you to choose among."

What Peach said was true. Meredith had a bevy of suitors to choose from . . . but unfortunately not one of them could hold a candle to the new Laney, and none of them, she knew—not even the Laney of her past—had touched both her heart and her soul as Laney had done this night when he kissed her in the gardens.

Julianne, meanwhile, sat with her gaze fastened to the window and the moon in the night sky above, and paid little mind to what Peach and Meredith were discussing.

She was composing a verse in her head, and she was thinking of Lord Thornwood.

Julianne had just experienced the most magical of nights, and it had been Lord Reginald Thornwood who'd made the evening seem as though it were sprinkled with fairy dust.

He'd mentioned he'd be at the balloon ascension later

in the week; the very one she and Meredith planned to attend. What a stroke of good fortune! Perhaps she'd have a chance to see him then, speak with him, maybe even walk with him.

Julianne continued staring up at the moon, and espied a single star shimmering near it. She made a wish on that star. A wish that began and ended with the handsome Lord Thornwood.

She couldn't wait to see him again.

Lord Reginald Thornwood left Lady Darcy's with an unsettled feeling in his gut. He couldn't help but wonder what had gone wrong on the dockside that night last July when he'd thought his hired miscreants had put an end to the lives of the sons of the second Earl of Graystone.

He'd been assured Laney had been shot and suffered a mortal wound by the lone vagabond he'd hired. And Larkin, according to the trio of thugs he'd paid dearly, had at the same time been done away with and then tossed into the river.

But Laney was very much alive.

Or Larkin was.

Thornwood, however, could not now be certain which twin had lived or died!

Whatever had happened, something had gone afoul. Laney—or Larkin—had persevered, and was now playing some dangerous cat-and-mouse game with him.

Thornwood scowled. He'd thought to be rid of both men, instead he was being haunted by one of them.

He glared up at the full moon that blared its light down on him as he waited for his carriage. Whatever was going on, Thornwood was determined to get to the bottom of it. And the lovely Miss Meredith Darlington was the one who would help him do so, even if *she* didn't know it.

She'd somehow captured the interest of the man claiming to be Lord Graystone, be that man Laney or Larkin. Whoever it was, Thornwood intended to use Miss Darlington to his advantage . . . for she alone could prove to be the enticing bait in the trap he was determined to set for the third Earl of Graystone. He'd thought to woo her and marry her, for her inheritance was staggering. But now, he decided she could be of better use to him as a pawn to get to Graystone. As for marrying an heiress, Miss Julianne Beveridge would do. She wasn't as rich, nor as pretty, but she was impressionable and obviously easily swayed by his charms.

Once his carriage arrived, Thornwood climbed inside and was glad enough to yank the curtains of the windows shut against the glow of moonlight.

It was the moon's light that forever reminded him of his hatred of the Graystone family for it was on a night such as this that his own spineless father had put a shot of lead into his brain, sullying the family name and leaving the lot of them in terrible debt—a huge portion of that debt owed to the Graystone family. A debt Thornwood still continued to pay.

But if Thornwood had his way, that debt of blood and money would soon be forgotten for he intended to bury it with the body of the man claiming to be the third Earl of Graystone. The spiteful second earl had created a clause in his will stating that upon the death of his last living son, all monies owed to Graystone family by the Thornwoods would be forgotten.

Lord Reginald Thornwood knew the reason why.

And he damned the man for it, and his sons as well.

* * *

Larkin, being the last to arrive at Lady Darcy's card-party, held true to his nature and was the first to leave the place. He spent an unmemorable few hours at his gentleman's club, and was livid to see that Reggie had made a recent wager at White's the previous evening. It was in this book that Larkin found too many wagers concerning the marriageable Miss Darlington—Thornwood's bet among them. He scowled as he spied the huge sum Reggie had wagered in being the very one to see "Miss D" to the altar.

So, that was Thornwood's plan; to marry Meredith, a very wealthy heiress, and take control of her inheritance.

Larkin felt his gut tighten, remembering how Meredith had taken a stroll with the duplicitous man. He wondered what they'd talked about . . . wondered, too, if Thornwood had touched her, kissed her, as he had done. B'god, if he had . . . !

Larkin, in a fury, headed out into the night, deciding what he needed more than another drink or further company was a good night's sleep, one void of any thoughts of Thornwood or even the beautiful Miss Meredith Darlington.

The moon's rays later mocked him as he headed up the grand outer steps of his brother's home in Grosvenor Square. He paused a moment on the threshold, staring up at the moon. The sight of it made him remember the past, and in particular that shining night before he'd been totally cut off from his family, and before his mother had died.

He had managed to lure Laney out for a night of riding hard on lathered horses. Together, they'd delivered some much-needed blunt to the destitute families of factory workers.

It had been Laney's first night of racing ill-gotten gains to the north. For Larkin, it had been a night like too many before it; he'd known in his heart that how he'd gotten the money was wrong. Knew, too, he would one day cease such recklessness. But being young and spirited and too caught up in the throes of the factory workers' misery, he'd tried to do what he could to aid them. He'd helped to feed a few children, clothe them, and perhaps, God willing, he'd helped give them something to hope for.

And for one exciting night, he and his brother had shared a bonding adventure. Larkin couldn't help but think that that night had made Laney question whether or not he wanted to continue on with the unfeeling legacy of the Graystone earls before him.

Alas, though, they'd not seen each other again after that night, for hours later their mother and father had argued. Larkin, and not Laney, overheard the hateful words their father had said to Amabel. Only Larkin had heard his mother's cries.

In the morning, Amabel was dead.

Larkin tried not to think about his beloved mother; he didn't want to recall how she'd met her end.

Instead, he tipped his face up to the moon's light, thinking of Laney, his precious brother who might or might not still live . . . and thinking of a female, very much alive, with amber eyes and a reckless spirit, a woman who obviously loved his brother as much as he did, and whom Larkin had agreed to marry.

He did not regret his decision to go along with Meredith's idea of matrimony. What he regretted was that it had been Laney's name, and not his own, that the enchanting Meredith whispered with such endearing sweetness, that it was Laney, and not he, whom Meredith so completely trusted.

The moon's light, whether to taunt him or to guide him, was the last thing Larkin saw as he later laid his head down upon a pillow his brother once slept upon and he tried to find sleep amid his tumbling thoughts.

Slumber, though, was long in coming.

When Larkin finally did fall asleep, his dreams were filled with the sight and scent of a woman he might soon marry but whom he could never again touch.

Could never again kiss.

And could certainly never call his own.

Dear God, but he would have to marry her in his brother's name, and then leave her untouched because of that fact. She would never be his because she loved another. Because she loved his brother—or rather, loved the memory of him.

And Thornwood, what of him? If Larkin wasn't careful, the evil Reggie would swoop in to snare the desirable Miss Meredith. The man would charm her and then deceive her.

Larkin solemnly swore to himself he wouldn't allow such a thing to happen. On the morrow, he would intensify his pursuit of the very marriageable Meredith. He told himself he would do so only for his brother's sake and also to save Meredith from a loveless union with the despicable Thornwood. Not once did he dare admit to himself he'd chosen such a course because of the kiss they'd shared and the feelings it had ignited in him.

Their shared kiss was best forgotten.

It *had* to be forgotten, Larkin sternly told himself, for

nothing could come of it . . . nothing but heartbreak, that is.

And there now existed one heart in this world—other than his dear brother's—Larkin did not wish to shatter. That heart belonged to Meredith Darlington.

Ten

Laney sat on a narrow cot, his back propped up against the wall with pillows and his legs stretched out in front of him. He had a perfect view of the moon in the night sky, framed as it was in the tiny window of the third-floor room he'd come to think of as home. Odd, but sight of the swollen moon reminded him of something, *someone*.

He didn't know who, though.

Laney shifted his gaze to the far corner of the room, spying the buff-colored breeches, expensive top hat, Weston-made coat, and high-polished Hessians he'd worn that night in July when he'd been shot.

Loving hands had repaired the garments, cleaning away the blood and dirt, and then had hung them in the corner, where they'd remained, untouched. The boots had been shined anew, then stuffed with clean rags to hold their shape for the day when Laney would once again walk in them. His shirt and neckcloth, he'd been told, had been irreparably ruined and so discarded.

Laney stared hard at the garments. They were the threads of a man with enough blunt to do as he pleased. He wondered why he didn't get a niggling feeling of memory when he looked at them.

How could a full moon affect him so, causing some elusive memory to whisk through his mind like a fleeting star, yet his own clothes could not bring one ounce of feeling to him? It was as though he'd never worn the garments; never wanted to.

Laney shook his head, sighing.

"Pray, do not torture yourself trying to remember," Wren whispered.

Laney looked to his left, smiling at Wren who sat upon a stiff-backed chair. A single taper burned on the table beside her. She looked lovely in the candlelight.

"How is it you always know what I am thinking?" he asked.

"It is not so difficult. Friends often know what the other is thinking—and the two of us have become friends, have we not?" she murmured, dropping her lashes and concentrating on the needle and thread she pulled through the rough fabric of the shirt she was mending for him.

"That we have," Laney quickly agreed, and was glad of the fact. The garment she so carefully mended was no doubt a castoff that once belonged to her friend, Jemmy. It had been Jemmy and several of his stout sailor friends along the docks who'd carried a wounded Laney to this very room that horrible night in July.

The lot of them had paid a visit just before they'd set sail on another ship, and Larkin had found himself liking Wren's friends. They'd played dice and had shared a bottle of gut-burning rum which had instantly made Laney dizzy in the head. Still, he'd had a good time listening to the men and their stories of life aboard ship.

What he'd liked best of all, though, was the fact Wren had sat near his cot, on a stool, and had laughed with him when he kept rolling lucky numbers with the dice. He'd never felt more free in his life, regardless of the fact he was still recovering from a festering wound.

Wren now lifted her gaze to his. "You aren't sorry, are you?"

"That we are now friends? Of course not!"

"No. That I brought you here."

Laney's green eyes softened. "You saved my life, Wren. For that I shall be forever grateful."

"But my room is small and cramped, and . . . ," she glanced once at the expensive garments, frowning, "and you obviously have been accustomed to finer things."

"Things I can't even recall," he reminded her.

"True, but the doctor said you will remember your past, in time. He said the absence of your memory is only temporary, a result of being shot and of the fever that claimed you. I—I only wished I'd had more coin and was able to pay for a physician more skilled than the one I brought to tend to you. After your wound festered, and the fever and the horrid delirium you suffered, I couldn't help but believe I'd done you a terrible injustice by bringing you here."

"Never say that, Wren," Laney insisted. "You did your best and I have lived to tell of the woeful tale. Indeed, my healing wound will one day become a scar that I can show my children and their children, and make them all ooh and ahh over the fact I was once set upon by a foul miscreant. No doubt they'll be all ears as I recount to them how a beauteous woman became my angel of mercy, gathering up her dockside friends and even a ship's surgeon to tend to my wound and make me whole again. They might even come to view me as one of Byron's corsairs."

Wren laughed then, as Laney had wanted her to do.

"You amaze me, Laney," she said. "The only memory you have is your first name and the fact you'd embarked upon a quest the night you were shot. And yet, here you are, wearing the castoffs of sailors, sitting atop a cot that is scarcely large enough to hold you, and being forced to endure the company of a woman whom you might not have even looked at twice in the past, and amazingly enough you seem, well . . . you seem . . . happy."

"I am," Laney insisted.

"I cannot fathom why."

"Mayhap it is because of you, Wren, your presence, your friendship."

Their gazes met and held across the small room. As always, Laney felt a tug of his heart whenever she looked at him and he at her. God, but she was gorgeous, and sweet, and sincere.

It was then, he realized, that he loved her.

"Come here," he said.

Wren shook her head. "I shouldn't. You need your rest. You need—"

"What I need is to feel you next to me, Wren." He patted the lumpy cot.

Wren knew she could deny him nothing. She put aside her sewing, stood up, smoothed her skirts, and then with a deep breath headed toward him.

Laney grinned as she tentatively eased down to sit on the cot. He reached for her left hand, threading his fingers through his. "There," he whispered. " 'Tis not so terrible, is it? Sitting beside me?"

"Of course not," she replied.

Indeed, Wren's heart soared at the nearness of him. She'd been aching to touch him of late, feeling a kind of pulsing need to be near him. But she'd been afraid of shattering the friendship they'd built, and there was the fact she did not want Laney to think any less of her. No true lady would ever share quarters with a man as Wren had done with Laney.

But Wren was no lady. She never had been.

And that was the problem.

Clearly, Laney was a gentleman, possibly even some fine swell. He didn't belong in her dreary room, did not belong mingling with sailors and a female who nearly sold her body and did sell her voice for a living.

Wren felt a tidal wave of guilt, for she liked Laney's company. They'd shared her books and their thoughts, and their time together had been pleasant and soothing once Laney's fever had passed.

But he didn't belong in her life, or she in his.

"Soon," Laney said, unmindful of her thoughts, "I shall leave this sickbed of mine. I should very much like to walk with you beneath a bonny sky. We'll go book hunting, maybe even house hunting. Would you like that?"

"I would," Wren admitted, but she knew they would never do such things. Before too long, Laney's memory would return, and he would leave her. He'd head for home, for the splendor and riches he'd left behind . . . and he'd want nothing to do with a dockside female such as she was.

Wren inwardly frowned as she squeezed Laney's hand, her heart all but bursting.

Laney returned the squeeze as well. "See that moon outside our window, Wren? It's a full moon, made for wishing and sharing dreams." He settled back on the pillows once again, feeling the tiredness he often had of late, but fighting it nonetheless. "Let us make some wishes of our own, shall we?"

He guided Wren back with him so that she, too, was positioned against the pillows she'd made for him.

"What is it you wish for?" she asked quietly, almost afraid to hear his answer.

"Contentment. A life filled with the peace I have known since I came awake in your cot."

"And your past?" she ventured, unable not to ask the question. "Do you not wish to know who and what you were?"

"Sometimes," he answered truthfully.

"But?"

Laney grinned, turning his face to hers and planting a quick kiss to her brow. "But I have to wonder what was so terribly wrong with that life to make me forget it. And the truth is, my life here with you has been exceedingly pleasant."

"Laney, you have spent more than half your time in the throes of a fever! How can you say it has been pleasant?"

"Because of you, my sweet Wren."

She stilled, turning her face to his. His eyes were so deep and so green she thought she would drown in their depths. When he pulled her face to his, she did not fight him.

"Ah, Wren," he murmured, "forgive me, but I cannot help myself." So saying, he claimed her lips with a light, thrilling kiss.

Wren unfolded to him like a flower hungry for water and sun. Their shared kiss turned passionate then, both of them giving and striving toward one another. His tongue darted inside her mouth, and Wren thought she would go mad with the pleasure of it all. *Here is goodness,* she thought, *here is love.*

Wren felt her toes curl and her heart soar. How she loved this man. She loved him with all her soul.

But she shouldn't.

He had no memory of his past—a past that was no doubt far above her meagerness. To love him would be to face a lowering setdown. Once he remembered his history, he would take flight, would speed far and fast away from her and her kind. He would laugh at the fact he'd been nursed by a female such as she was. He would not give her a backward glance once he resumed his wealthy life.

Wren drew back from Laney's lips. "You should rest," she said, breathless and nervous. "I've kept you awake long enough."

Laney reluctantly let her go, knowing he shouldn't have kissed her, should not have frightened her with his overpowering need of her.

"Yes," he said. "I suppose I should. I grow weary of being the invalid, yet the only way to escape such bonds is to rest and heal quickly."

Wren stood up, running a trembling hand across her mouth that was still moist with the taste of him. "Yes. Rest, Laney. Get some sleep."

She headed back to her corner chair where she again took up needle and thread and the coarse shirt she'd been mending.

Laney watched her retreat, a wry grin on his handsome lips. Once he was well again, he knew, he would make the woman his.

"Goodnight, Wren," he whispered, making a show of settling down on the bed and closing his eyes.

Wren bent her head, concentrating on her stitches. "Goodnight, Laney."

* * *

She waited until she thought he was asleep. Only then did she blow out the candle. She waited, in the moon's light slanting through the grimy window, for some sign that Laney was truly sleeping before she gently laid her mending aside and got to her feet.

She hated leaving him like this. Always had. But she had a job to do. She couldn't afford to pay rent, buy candles, and the vegetables they'd lived on if she did not go to work. If not for her meager pay, she and Laney would be out on the street.

Too, she owed Jemmy's friend, the ship's surgeon who had so willingly helped them, several more payments for his work in extracting the ball of lead from Laney's shoulder and seeing him through his fever. She now had a mountain of bills to pay, most of them stemming from the fact she'd taken on the wounded Laney. The shirts he wore didn't come for free, and the food he needed to replenish his strength had cost her dearly.

Wren wasn't complaining. She loved Laney. Loved him more than her own life. She'd go to work and pay their bills, and she'd cherish every moment she had with him.

But she didn't know what she'd do once he regained his full memory.

The future was precarious at best, always had been, and she'd not be ruining the present with thoughts of what it might bring. For the moment, Laney was here with her.

And he'd kissed her!

In the darkness, Wren once again felt her mouth tingle from his remembered kiss. If Laney eventually left her for his former life—and he would, she had no doubt—she would have her memories of him. She was not a greedy creature. She would treasure what they'd shared. For all her life, she would remember him.

Like a thief in the night, Wren gathered up her threadbare cloak and then headed out of the room, the latch falling in place behind her.

Wren hurried down the stairs and out into the street. The conveyance she'd hired earlier stood waiting. Hood drawn up, she ran for it.

"Hurry," she ordered the driver. "Make haste for Madame Blue's."

"Aye," the toothy man obliged.

With a creak of carriage wheels, the conveyance sped off, leaving Wren's decrepit boardinghouse and her handsome gentleman friend behind. She was heading for a secretive life she wanted no one to know about.

To the men who frequented Madame Blue's less than illustrious establishment, Wren was known simply as "Mistress of the Night." They came to hear her voice, view her body . . . and perhaps have a taste of her sweet nectar.

For the first time in a long while, Wren hated going there. She looked out the window of the carriage just as they rounded a turn . . . and she thought she saw Laney's face staring down at her.

How absurd.

Laney was fast asleep.

He had no knowledge of her night life.

God willing, he never would.

Laney, having heaved himself off the cot when he realized Wren had slipped out of the room again, forced his weak limbs over to the window. He stood back a pace or two, not wanting her to view him in the moon's light that poured into the chamber.

Silently, he watched as she headed for a hired hackney, spoke a few words to the driver, and then climbed inside the carriage.

Within a moment, she was gone.

But to where? And why?

Laney had no answers.

He leaned against the wall, his brow wet with perspiration. He felt dizzy and sick from his quick movements, but he forced the feelings down. He was determined to become whole again . . . and just as determined to claim Wren as his own. She'd be back come dawn, just as she always was.

This time though, Laney would be awake and waiting for her.

He headed for the cot and a sleepless night. He and his angel of mercy had much to discuss come sunrise.

Eleven

Dawn was breaking as Wren hurried out the back entrance of Madame Blue's, quickly opened the gate, and scurried through it to the crowded alley there. She didn't slow her pace until she'd gotten a block away, threaded around the buildings, and then came out on the street just beside her favorite bakery. Only then she did pause a moment to catch her breath and push back a curl of her blond hair.

Every time she left that horrid house, she felt as though someone would try and stop her, would make her go back inside, upstairs, to do what the other girls at Madame Blue's did every night for the many male guests.

Wren shivered in the cool morning air, drawing her worn cloak more closely about her. She tried to calm her nerves.

She was getting too fidgety of late. The reason was Laney. She hated leaving him every night for a job she despised but could not exist without.

Wren stepped inside the bakery. Bess, the baker's gray-haired wife, was just setting out some hot buns and a few sweetcakes as well. "Good morning," Wren called in greeting.

Bess, her apron covered with flour, beamed at the sight

of her friend. "You be here earlier than usual, dearie," she said.

"Am I? I—I hadn't noticed."

"Earlier and earlier, every day," Bess remarked as Wren struggled over how many sweetcakes she could afford to purchase. "I be thinking you have some reason to hurry home these days. You haven't gone and got yourself married, have you?"

Wren suddenly stilled. She shook her head. "No," she answered softly. "I haven't."

"But you've got a secret you're keeping. I can see that much. Here now, don't you be worrying over what you can afford to buy this morning. I'm in a right sunny mood today. Haven't a clue why I should be, I only know that I am." She wrapped up a half-dozen sweetcakes, and a loaf of fresh bread, and a few buns as well and then pressed them into Wren's hands before another word was said.

Wren stared down at the bundle. "I—I can't take all of this, Bess."

"Nonsense. Of course you can. I insist." Bess gave her a wink. "And I won't be worried that any of it will go to waste, seeing as how you've been buying more of our goods than usual. Either you've grown a huge appetite, or well . . . like I said, you've got a secret you're keeping."

Wren murmured her thanks, grateful for Bess's kindness. It took too much of Wren's money to hire a carriage to transport her to Madame Blue's each night, but she was afraid to walk the dark streets alone. The morning, though, was not such a frightful time and she was able to walk home to her boardinghouse. Still, the one carriage ride a day cost her dearly, leaving little money for any other food than was necessary.

"You're a true friend, Bess," Wren said. "I won't ever forget your kindness."

"No need to be thanking me. Now you just hurry on home, you hear? I don't like the thought of you out and about on your own."

Wren wanted very much to confide in the older woman and tell her she was no longer alone. But she couldn't. Someone had tried to murder Laney. Of course, it could have been a random thief thinking to rob him . . . but then again, the happening could have far deeper meaning. Seeing for herself the fine cut of Laney's clothes, hearing his cultured speech and knowing for a fact what a supreme gentleman he was, Wren deduced the shooting on the dock was the work of someone who wished to see him dead. She couldn't breathe a word of Laney's presence to anyone—not even Bess.

Wren headed back out onto the street. The sun had completely risen, and its rays slanted down, beaming a warm light between the many buildings. A few shopkeepers were sweeping brooms across the stoops of their stores, and a flower girl was already setting out her wares to be sold for the day. To Wren's right, a mail coach whizzed past, the driver slapping his whip above his frisky team. In the opposite direction came a lumbering wagon laden with produce and heading for the market.

Wren loved the city, loved the smells and sights and sounds of it—especially in the morning, when her work was done. With each new morning, she always felt as if this might possibly be the day in which she could turn her back on Madame Blue's and never return there. It was a foolish thought, she knew, but one she had every time she walked home.

She supposed the fact her prospects did not seem so depressing was the reason she held hope a change would soon come; if one didn't have any hope, then how could one deal with the pain of grim reality? But there *was* hope, she told herself now.

There was Laney.

Thinking of him buoyed her spirits more, and on impulse she bought a small posy from the flowergirl. Pressing the white, delicate blooms to her nose, Wren headed for home and for the man who'd brightened her life.

Laney spent a long, fitful night pacing the small room, wondering where Wren had gone, what she was doing—and with whom. What reasons could a young, beautiful woman have for spending each night away from her own bed?

The possibilities were far from pleasant.

Feelings of betrayal began to worm their way through Laney's soul . . . and that sense of being betrayed reminded him of something, *someone,* yet he couldn't quite grasp the entire memory, all of which only served to agitate him further.

Had Wren betrayed him this night, and all the other nights? Had she been with another man? With more than one man? True, he held no claim to her other than the friendship they'd forged, but he thought she understood how deeply he'd come to care for her. Had thought, too, they'd become so close as not to deceive the other.

By five A.M., Laney's mind was in a rage, his heart eaten with jealousy. He paced until his wounded arm burned and cramped. He paced until he thought he'd go mad. He was tired and gritty-eyed from lack of sleep. Still, though, he paced.

And waited.

And wondered.

He was dressed when Wren finally entered the room an hour later. She appeared startled to see him awake, even more startled to find him dressed in his own breeches, coat, and polished Hessians. The coarse, linen shirt he wore beneath the fine coat was the very one she'd mended for him the night before. It had been the first thing he'd put on, and he'd felt an odd tumult of love and betrayal when he'd smelled her delicate scent that clung to the fabric.

His Wren . . . she was his, yet she stole away every night, to do God knew what! Jealousy, worry, anger tumbled through him at the sight of her. He must have looked like Lucifer incarnate, for she immediately stilled.

"Laney," she whispered.

"Good morning, Wren." His voice was just a husk of a sound.

"I—I'd thought you'd be asleep," she said, finally rousing herself to move. She closed the door softly behind her, a wary look in her gaze.

"Thought . . . or hoped?"

"I beg your pardon?"

"Tell me where you have been, Wren."

She let out a soft breath, shaking her head as though she didn't understand the meaning of his question. "I—I went to the bakery, and then I bought some flowers and—"

"Prior to all of that."

"Laney . . . please, you—you've never questioned me like this before."

"I am questioning you now."

Though he hadn't intended to do so, Laney found himself closing the distance between them. Again, the feelings of anger, betrayal, even abandonment pumped through him as he came to stand directly in front of Wren.

Abandoned . . . yes, that is what he felt, and he knew in that instant that someone in his past, someone just as dear to him as Wren was now, had abandoned him. Lord help him, but he wouldn't suffer such abandonment again! He took hold of her shoulders, backing her against the door.

"Laney," she gasped, frightened. "Don't, Laney. Please don't do this."

He was deaf to her words. His ears rang only with the pounding rage of his soul. "Tell me, Wren. Tell me now how and where you have been spending your nights."

She tried to pull away from him, but Laney, in his blind jealousy, wouldn't allow it. Instead, he pinned her fast to the wall, not caring that she dropped the posy she'd been carrying and the wrapped bundle as well. All he could see, all he could feel, was Wren's duplicity. She smelled of morning sun and fresh air . . . and faintly of cigar smoke and a scent that could be nothing other than a man's smell.

Laney felt the knot in his gut tighten even more. He didn't like the fiend he'd suddenly become, but he was powerless to stop himself from demanding answers from her.

He took her delicate chin in his hand, forcing her to look him directly in the eyes. "The truth," he demanded. "I would have it now . . . or else—"

"Or else what?" she cried, coming to life, her eyes

filling with tears. "You will hurt me? Beat me like some lowly beast? Is that what you will do, Laney?"

"I will have an answer, dammit!"

She winced as his hold tightened, and then, suddenly, she steeled herself, glaring up at him. "I have known the banefulness of a father's hatred, known too the sting of the back of his hand . . . and worse." A sob caught in her throat when Laney went stock still. "Oh, yes, I have known *that*," she whispered, her tears coming unchecked.

Laney was thunderstruck. "Dear God in heaven," he rasped. He felt suddenly as though the wind had been knocked out of him. "Ah, Wren—"

"No," she snapped, jerking away when he would have touched her cheek with softness. "You demand answers from me, and you shall have them!"

"Not like this. I have done you wrong in both word and deed by approaching you in such anger. I never meant—"

She shook her head, determined to have her say, to tell him everything about her.

"I—I am no lady, Laney. I have never had hope of being one. I am merely the daughter of a governess who found what she thought was love in the arms of a titled son. He took his pleasure of her and then stood silent while she was forced out of her employment for loving too freely, too trustingly. Her reputation was ruined, and she had a baby—me—growing inside of her when she found herself alongside the docks, with no money and no hope."

"Wren, please, you don't have to—"

"I do, Laney. Let me finish. My—my mother was very beautiful; it did not take long before she caught the eye of another man, a sailor. He was kind, at first, or so I was told. But later, after I was born and it became clear I would favor my father in looks, he began to truly hate me. When I got older and Mama taught me to read, write, to sing and play an instrument, he claimed I was taking on airs, said I would bring us all into debt for the coins she spent on teaching me. He claimed I needed to be taught my place in life. I remember the first time he beat me; I—I was five years old. I felt ancient after that.

"Then Mama died and I didn't have her to protect me anymore . . . and—and he decided he didn't like bruises on my skin, so he marked me in other ways." Wren squeezed her eyes tight and turned her face away from him. Her words drifted off, muddled by her wracking sobs.

After a long moment, she added, "He—he died a few years ago, by his own hand. And though I should have felt sorry for a man who could take his own life, I—I only knew anger that he'd planned his death in a way that *I* would be the one to find his lifeless body. He left me in debt, having sold off everything of value my mother ever owned. I—I didn't have many choices. I could read and write and sing and play instruments, but what good was all of that when I had no sterling reputation? I had little prospects and the threat of debtor's prison loomed above me . . . until I learned of a certain place where a woman with any smattering of an education and a fair face would be welcomed. I found employment in a house known for its beautiful women and the pleasures men can find there. Though I've never actually had to . . . entertain the many male guests with my body, I do play the pianoforte and sing for them." She looked at him, her eyes filled with tears. "That is what I do, Laney. That is how I pay for my room and my food and the few gowns I purchase. So if you intend to hurt me or—or even hate because of all this, then that will have to be your choice. But know that I've been hurt by men too many times in the past. I—I cannot suffer it any longer."

Laney felt a fiend. He was appalled at all Wren had had to endure, and even more sickened by his own behavior.

How could he have frightened her like this? Never, in his life, had he ever hurt another person.

But he'd hurt someone now. He'd hurt the woman he loved . . . a young woman who had been wronged too many times in the past. Laney thought he'd die at the sight of her tears.

"Dear, sweet Wren," he whispered. "I don't hate you. Never could I hate you. You've worked in that house because you had no choice. I will not stand in judgment of your choices."

She flinched once more as he moved to touch her.

"Ah, Wren," he murmured, her name passing his lips as a whisper, "I am so sorry. Forgive me. Please, please, forgive me, my love. I didn't mean to hurt you. I never intended to hurt you. I—I don't know what has come over me. I only know that I . . . I love you. I love you, Wren, and I don't ever want to lose you!"

Tentative, she looked up at him, joy beginning to take over the pain etched on her lovely, tear-streaked features. Slowly, almost hesitantly, she moved into the embrace he offered.

Laney gathered her into his arms. It didn't matter where she'd been or who she'd seen during the past night. What mattered was right here and right now—and Wren was here, and he loved her. God, how he loved her.

They slid down against the door, both of them dropping to their knees as Laney rained soft, tender kisses on her brow, her temples, her cheeks, her mouth, their tears mingling.

"Sweet Wren. Forgive me. Forgive me," he murmured. "All I ever want to do is love you. Never hurt you. Can you believe that, even in the face of my horridness?"

She nodded, touching her fingers to each side of his face as she returned his kisses.

"I have been an ogre," he rasped.

"No. Never that." She gave a tremulous smile, touching her nose to his. "You are the man who loves romance, are you not?"

He kissed her mouth. "But I've had too little romance, as have you," he said against her lips. "No more, though. No more, do you hear?"

"Yes."

"We shall have a lifetime of romance. I shall do everything in my power to make you forget the horrible moments of your past. Indeed, I shall make it my quest."

"You would do that . . . for me?"

"Only for you."

She melted against him, loving the feel of him, finding safety in his arms.

They remained there, holding each other for a long while, and watched as the sun's light grew stronger in the window. Carriages could be heard rattling over the street below. Hawkers began shouting their wares. The world was coming alive, but for Laney and Wren, the world consisted merely of the tiny room and their bodies pressed tight together.

Laney lovingly caressed her. "I think," he whispered,

"that today should be the start of a better world for us. We shall begin anew, you and I."

"I—I'd like that, Laney."

He grinned. "What say you we take a walk? I have lingered in this room for too long. I need fresh air, to feel the sun on my face, and to have the woman I love strolling on my arm."

Wren sat up, pushing a strand of hair from her eyes. "Do you think that's wise, to be out and about? I mean, someone tried to—to . . . ," she faltered.

"Murder me," he finished when he realized she couldn't say the word. "Well, I'd like to see them try to do so again. You see, my lovely Wren, I now have a purpose in life. Indeed, I have *you* in my life, and I am feeling wildly invincible."

Her brow creased with worry. "Still, though, I don't think you should risk it. Whoever tried to harm you might do so again."

"And mayhap it was all a random sort of thing. Perhaps I was just in the wrong place at the wrong time." He got to his feet, reaching out with his good arm to help her up as well. "Whatever happened is in the past. I shall no longer hide in this room, being the invalid and leaving our financial woes to you. It is high time I took care of my lady . . . and you are that, Wren. Never doubt it. *You are my lady.*"

Wren allowed him to guide her upright, tears threatening to overtake her again as he touched her chin, his fingers caressing their way to the shell of her right ear.

"I am going to create a future for us, Wren," Laney promised. "One that is bright and beautiful and never ending, and one in which the only shadows we see are the ones we create upon a candle-lit wall. I want to grow old with you, my sweet Wren. I want to greet each day with you at my side and end each day with you in my arms."

Her face beamed. "I can think of nothing I'd like more."

"Very well, then. Dry your eyes, and let us head out into the sunlight."

Wren didn't need to be told twice. Before long, she and Laney were outside. They walked and talked and spent a leisurely morning watching the barges on the river. They spoke of everything . . . and nothing. The world was suddenly a magical place; it was wide and wondrous, filled with possibilities one minute, and then just as quickly cozy and private, with just the two of them alive and in love.

Wren had brought along the sweetcakes and rolls Bess had given her. They shared their treat with each other and also with the birds. Wren was feeling light of heart when they finally headed back to the boardinghouse.

It was then she had the distinct feeling someone was watching them, following them. She glanced over her shoulder, catching sight of a man dressed in a seaman's garb, his slouch hat nearly covering one eye. He paused as she caught his gaze, then quickly lowered his hat and made a pretense of staring out at the river, as though something of interest had taken his fancy.

Wren wasn't fooled. He'd been trailing them. Could he, possibly, be the one who'd shot Laney? Did he intend to finish what he'd begun that night on the docks.

Wren's heartbeat quickened. She felt ill at ease. Her hand tightened over Laney's arm.

"Something the matter, love?" he asked, smiling at her.

Wren shook her head. "No, I . . . uh, I am just so very thirsty. All the walking we've done has made me feel quite parched." She guided him into a chophouse they were passing.

The place was very busy—just as Wren hoped it would be—and she and Laney had to navigate their way through the smoke-filled front room.

"Wren, I don't think we should have come in here," Laney said, balking at the sight of so many seamen. The only women present were a few buxom barmaids, their smiles wide and saucy and their minds on things other than the drinks they served.

Wren didn't stop moving. "Yes, I—I suppose you are correct, Laney," she said, relaxing somewhat as they were swallowed up in the midst of the many rowdy sailors. A few were bold enough to grin at her. Wren purposefully ignored them, tugging Laney along until they stumbled into the kitchens.

A maid frowned at them. "If yer worryin' about yer food, just have some patience. I be preparin' it as fast as I can."

"Don't worry about that," said Wren. "Just tell me, is there a back way out of here? I—I fear the commotion out front is too much for us. We would just like to leave."

The maid looked relieved she would have two less meals to prepare. She motioned with a nod of her head to the door behind her. "A way out is right in front of you. Now hurry and begone. Yer in my way."

Wren was only too eager to oblige. She headed for the door, a perplexed Laney moving alongside her.

"Wren, what the blazes was all that about?" he asked, once they were in the alley.

Wren didn't relax until the door had latched firmly

behind them. She gave Laney her brightest smile, told him she was sorry she'd been so silly as to have pulled him into such a place, and then hurried him along.

"I guess I lost my head for a moment," she explained.

"I should say so," he said. He paused a moment, pulling her to a stop with him. "Could it be the happiness we've discovered in each other has caused us both to be a bit out of sorts?" he asked, pulling her into his embrace.

Wren melted against him. "Yes," she murmured, suddenly hypnotized by his gaze. "I suppose it has."

He grinned, kissed the tip of her nose, then grinned some more. "I'd follow you anywhere, Wren . . . even into a seamy chophouse."

He rubbed his cheek lovingly against hers, and Wren thought she would go mad with wanting him. But she had to get him away from the man who was following them.

She pulled back, slowly, provocatively. Unable to think of any other ploy to hurry him away from the alley, she said, "If you are considering kissing me again, then you will have to catch me first." With that, she slipped out of his hold and then hurried away, though not as quickly as she'd wanted to do so. She knew he was still recovering from his wound. She couldn't very well expect him to dash after her.

But Laney surprised her, setting a fast pace.

Wren turned and made a dash through the alley, and then to the street, where Laney finally came abreast of her. He was laughing as he caught her.

Wren laughed, too, when she saw no one was following them. They'd managed to elude the man who'd been trailing them.

Together, they headed for home.

Twelve

Laney, Wren realized, had tired from his sleepless night and their morning's walk. She insisted that he rest. She sat beside the cot on her little stool, reading to him from a book of poetry her mother had given her years ago. She told him about the day she'd been gifted with the book.

"She loved poetry," Wren said. "And music." She slanted him a shy smile. "And romance, too."

Laney reached for her hand, his eyes heavy-lidded. "She should be the one part of your past we never allow to be forgotten."

Wren nodded, her gratitude evident. How sweet he was. After a moment of silence she asked, "And what of your past, Laney? How can we go forward without knowing the truth? How can *you* go forward?"

" 'Tis simple. I have you now. You are all I need. You are the sum total of my happiness. I have no need of a past."

Wren was not so certain. Her gaze shifted to his fine coat, even his expensive boots. "Are you not the least bit curious?"

"At times," he admitted, finally closing his eyes and allowing his weariness to overtake him.

"So?"

"So what, my love?"

"One of us should at least try and discover who and what you were before that night on the docks when I found you. My goodness, Laney, you might even be—be married for all we know."

His eyes flew open, and then he let them drift shut again, smiling as he caught sight of her face. "Ah, no. Never that. I cannot be married for I fell in love with you too fast and too easily for that. I can't explain it, but I think I was very lonely in my past . . . and abandoned, and betrayed.

"Yes, I was that. I am certain of it," he said. "Which is the reason why I reacted so violently when you were gone all night, and all the nights prior. I hated that feeling of possible betrayal and abandonment . . . hated to think you might be with someone else."

Wren leaned forward. "I swear to you, Laney, I only sang and played instruments for the men in that horrid place I've gone to these past nights. No man has touched me, other than—"

"Shhh," he soothed, his hand seeking hers, his fingers twining with her own. "What that despicable man did was low and vile, but is in no way a reflection of you. You were wronged. You'll never be wronged again. Never. I swear to God."

His hand closing over hers gave Wren strength, and a purpose.

"I shall not leave you for another night again, Laney," she vowed passionately. "Tonight—and every night, if that is your wish—I shall be only with you."

"It *is* my wish, Wren. And my hope, and my joy, and the very thing that shall make me whole again."

She believed him.

Both of them fell silent, enjoying their closeness and the solitude. Hours might have slipped past, or maybe just a few minutes.

He was falling asleep, Wren realized. But she had something more to say before he drifted into slumber, something to tell him.

"Laney?"

"Hmmm?"

She wanted to tell him there was something she must do this day, wanted to tell him she had to cut all ties to her past, and be paid the money Madame Blue owed her for her wages. She needed the funds because without them she and Laney would know true difficulty in the coming days.

But though these were the words she wished to say, she did not say them. She knew he would most likely gainsay her, insisting she'd not go anywhere near that despicable house.

So instead, Wren simply told him she needed to purchase some goods.

"I—I shan't be gone long," Wren whispered. "I'll be back before the dinner hour and will bring you something good and nourishing to eat. Perhaps some wine, too. We'll have our own little feast tonight. Would you like that?"

He nodded, though just barely. Wren frowned, worrying over him. He'd been up all night, fretting when he should have been resting. That she, too, had been awake for hours was not to be counted; she was accustomed to little sleep, and she certainly hadn't been shot and left to bleed to death on the docks. He'd suffered an ordeal. That he'd suffered from wounds of the soul last night was something Wren wouldn't soon forget. He'd said he'd been betrayed and abandoned in the past. By whom, she wondered, and why?

Wren eased back from his bedside, a determined set to her features. She knew what she had to do this day. She must return to Madame Blue's, obtain her money, and then inform the vile woman she would no longer be employed as a singer.

Wren waited until she could hear the sounds of Laney's deep breathing before she eased off the stool. She wondered if he'd even heard her when she'd said she was going to head out and buy some food for them. In the event that he had really heard her words, she wanted to leave him a note, but she had no paper.

She decided to use the front page of the book of poetry. That done, she laid the book upon the stool beside the cot, marking the page with the posy she'd dropped when Laney had confronted her earlier that day.

She gathered up her cloak and hurried out the door.

By the time Wren reached Madame Blue's, she found that the woman was not in residence but had gone to the butcher shop; the last delivery of meat had been less than acceptable to her and she trusted no servant to ensure that the next delivery was adequate.

Wren's request to meet with her was denied, and no time was given for when she might expect a meeting.

Wren wasn't pleased. She and Laney desperately needed her wages. The rent was due, and unfortunately Wren had barely enough funds to buy them her promised "feast" for this evening. Come tomorrow, they would have no food to eat, and she would have no employment.

She was in a decidedly brown mood as she sat alone

in the side parlor Madame Blue used as an office. Wren jumped to her feet when she heard the latch lift and the door ease open. She hoped to confront her employer, but it wasn't Madame Blue who entered. It was Suzanne, one of the girls who worked abovestairs.

The young woman was about the same age as Wren. She wasn't as sultry in looks as many of the other women who plied their trade in the rooms above, instead she had a very delicate beauty and was a favorite of the many male guests who came every night seeking various sport. Suzanne and Wren had not talked overly much. When the woman wasn't busy with her customers, she spent her time with her young son, Willy, who also lived in the house but had a bedchamber near the kitchens.

Suzanne frowned when she saw Wren. "Are you waiting to speak with Madame Blue?"

"I am," Wren replied, "but I don't expect her soon. In fact, I don't expect her at all." Wren noticed the young woman was actually shaking and that her eyes were redrimmed. "What is wrong, Suzanne? You're trembling. And you've been crying." Wren felt a horrid sick feeling in the pit of her stomach. Who knew what transpired in the rooms above the stairs? Who knew what the quiet Suzanne had been forced to endure? "Sweet Lord," Wren whispered. "You haven't been hurt, have you?"

Suzanne's eyes filled with more tears. "No. I've not been physically hurt." Quietly, she closed the door behind her then lowered her face, her shoulders quivering with her soft cries. "You weren't supposed to be here, Wren. No one was. I—I'd intended to come in here and . . . and do something I shouldn't."

"Do what?" Wren asked.

Suzanne's tortured gaze met Wren's. Slowly, Suzanne

lifted her left hand, uncurled her fingers and showed Wren a key she'd been clutching. "This opens Madame Blue's strongbox. She keeps things in this box; names of her employees—former and present—pin money, and trinkets the guests sometimes give to her." Suzanne shook her head, clearly at odds with her thoughts. "I—I was intending to open that box and take what is rightfully mine. I haven't been paid in weeks, Wren. None of the girls abovestairs have. And my Willy, he—he needs a new pair of shoes, and . . . and he's getting older. Soon he'll be old enough to puzzle out what his mother does every night. I don't want him to know. I don't want him to *ever* know." Her tears almost choked her, but she kept talking, clearly relieved to share her woes with someone. "So I thought I'd take the wages due me and any written proof that I'd ever worked here and—and just flee, me and Willy. I can't live here anymore, Wren. I can't go up those stairs and do what I've been doing for the past four years. I just can't!"

"Then don't," Wren said. "Open the strongbox. Take what's due you. I'll never breathe a word of it, I swear to you."

"You'd do that for me?"

Wren nodded, a knot of hatred hardening inside of her at what the vile Madame Blue had done to Suzanne, and to Willy and to so many others—and even to herself. She'd trapped them. Made them her slaves, in a sense. And poor little Willy, a boy of barely five years, was living in such a disreputable place . . . it was unforgivable. "Open the box," Wren urged.

Suzanne hesitated. "I want to but I'm afraid."

"Why? You'll only be taking what's owed to you, and then you and Willy will be free."

"But then what?" Suzanne whispered. "You know as well as I that Madame Blue has connections with government officials." Suzanne shuddered. "You've seen with your own eyes how many men of Parliament secretly enter these doors and then head to some private room."

"Surely none would be so foolish as to publicly support the woman," Wren replied.

"No, but they'd do it privately. She could find me with great ease, I've no doubt of that! And Willy . . . he could be taken away from me. I could be sent to prison, or worse—"

"Suzanne," Wren said forcibly, "do you honestly believe Madame Blue would go to all that trouble if you took only what is due you? She might even be glad that you've gone and taken your son with you. You are indeed a favorite here, but," she added with a frown, "there is always someone new being lured into this life. You know it's true."

Suzanne nodded. "Yes. I know." She drew in a ragged breath. "But if I leave . . . what then? How will I manage? I have no skills. You, Wren, can sing and play an instrument, and you can read and write. I—I can do none of those things."

"There must be something," Wren whispered, though she had no answers. She, herself, was facing the grim reality of leaving a steady wage.

Suzanne surprised her then, saying, "Yes, I—I suppose I do have a choice, but I'm afraid I let that choice slip away from me today."

"What are you talking about, Suzanne?"

After a moment of hesitation, she said, "There is something called the Midnight Society. They've offered

Willy and me a place to live just so long as I don't work *here.* A few months ago, one of the newer girls left when the same society offered her help. I don't know what became of her, only that she got out."

"So why don't you accept their aid?" Wren asked.

Suzanne frowned, a tormented look in her eyes. "Because I'm afraid to trust them, to trust anyone. And . . . and because it was a man who came to me with the offer." Suzanne gave a short, mirthless laugh. "Imagine, me, being afraid of some white-haired man. But I was. Truth is, I am frightened by *any* man. And besides, if this society was truly good and if they did help me and Willy for a short time, what then? I still would have no employment and no way of taking care of my son."

Wren knew there weren't any easy answers. Not for either of them. Of a sudden, before she lost her nerve, she took the key out of Suzanne's palm. "Show me where the strongbox is, Suzanne."

Suzanne looked alarmed. "Why?"

"Because I'm going to open it, and then you'll take what rightfully belongs to you and Willy . . . and I'll take what is mine."

Suzanne shook her head. "No, Wren. We shouldn't. We could make things far worse for us, we—"

"Worse?" Wren's features hardened. "I cannot imagine anything worse than having to work in this despicable place for one minute longer. No," she said. "We're going to get ourselves free of this place. And then you, Suzanne, will take Willy and head for the safe place the Midnight Society has offered you. For once in our lives we're going to do something for *us,* do you hear?"

Suzanne, looking fearful, only nodded. "In the cabinet," she whispered. "The strongbox is in the cabinet."

Wren turned, then headed for the cabinet. The box wasn't much larger than a book, but it was heavy. She slid the key into the lock, turned it, then popped open the lid. Wren's heart fell. There were a few notes and coins, but not nearly enough to equal the money due the two of them. Wren began counting the notes.

Suzanne paled as Wren pressed the bulk of them into her hands. "Here," said Wren. "This is yours. You've certainly earned it."

"I—I don't know. Now that I am actually here and the box has been opened, I—I don't think I can take the money. I am no thief, Wren"

"Nor am I. But then again, I'd never thought I'd be working in a brothel one day." Wren pressed the money into Suzanne's shaking hands. "Just take it. Don't think twice. You have a son to care for. And besides, as I've said, the money is owed to you."

"But what about you?" Suzanne gasped. "Surely what is left is hardly what is due to you."

Suzanne was correct. It wasn't. But Wren was no longer worrying so much about herself as she was thinking of Suzanne and little Willy. "It is enough," Wren said. "I merely sing for my wages, Suzanne. Madame Blue isn't so generous with my pay."

Suzanne stared down at the contents of the box, seeing the sheaf of notes there, and a small silver pendant and its chain as well.

"Take the pendant," she urged.

Wren didn't want to, but then again, the sphere was clearly fashioned of pure silver and had been created by a skilled craftsman, and the chain was heavy and well made. Wren scooped it up before she could change her mind. She looped it about her neck, and let the sphere drop down beneath her gown, and prayed for forgiveness.

There now remained only the many sheafs of paper.

Suzanne looked nervously at the pages. "What is written upon them?" she demanded, surprising Wren with her intensity.

Wren rifled through the pages, frowning. "Just what you suspected. 'Tis the names, the ages, the hair and eye color and a detailed description of all those who work here. There are even dates of employment," answered Wren.

"Burn them!" Suzanne begged.

Wren pulled out only the pages that referred to herself and to Suzanne. "I don't know what the others want, and I'm not about to interfere in their lives. I will, though, take whatever reference is made to us." She handed Suzanne several pages, all of them documenting the young woman's employment. As for the pages detailing her own history with Madame Blue, Wren rolled them up and then tucked them up one sleeve of her gown.

Wren then snapped the box shut, locked it and replaced it in the cabinet. She handed the key back to Suzanne.

"I—I don't know what to say," Suzanne whispered.

"You don't have to say anything," Wren replied. "Now go on. Gather up your things and Willy and get out of this place."

"But what about you?" Suzanne asked.

Wren thought of Laney. "I'll be fine," she murmured. "Just fine. No matter what."

Suzanne, clearly at odds over what she and Wren had just done, said nothing and then, still trembling, left the room.

Wren watched her leave. She had to wonder if Suzanne would actually be able to gather enough courage to leave the brothel for good. "Godspeed," Wren whispered, wishing only good things for Suzanne and little Willy. And then she, too, hastened out of the office. She did not wish to meet with Madame Blue now.

Once she was out on the street, Wren again had the feeling someone was watching her, following her. She glanced back. It wasn't a man dressed as a seaman she espied hovering a block behind her, but another man. This one was big, dark-haired, and wore a brown coat and breeches . . . and he didn't turn away when her gaze met his.

Wren's blood turned to ice in her veins, knowing she was most likely being followed because she'd been seen with Laney. How many people were watching and waiting for Laney? Who was he that there was such interest in his whereabouts?

Wren considered halting her steps, turning about and confronting the man. But she didn't dare. She felt a keen desire to be far and fast away from him.

So thinking, she picked up her pace, darted out into the street, between the many carriages, and then lost herself on the other side, scurrying between buildings, threading her way through alley after alley, and finally reaching the street of her boardinghouse, alone.

Wren forced herself to calm down enough to purchase some wine, cheese, a loaf of bread, and two fresh apples. She had promised Laney a "feast," and she intended to bring him something good to eat.

She entered the boardinghouse with the feeling that no one had followed her; she'd managed to elude yet another follower.

Laney was awake when she entered the room. This time, though, he was not angry.

"I found your note," he said softly, rising to greet her with a warm hug. "And I see you've brought the promised food. Soon, my love, I shall be the one to see to our welfare."

"I don't mind," Wren replied, reveling in the feel of his arms about her.

"But I do mind," he said. He released her, took the many packages, and then made quick work of laying the food out on the tiny, single table of the room. Wren, meanwhile, pulled out the pages she'd stolen from Madame Blue's strongbox. She hid them in the book she'd left for Laney, then turned, glad to see he was still busy with the food.

Once he was finished, Laney swept one arm wide toward the small table, executed a bow that was both ridiculous, considering their circumstances, and touching in its sincerity.

"Dear Laney," Wren said, smiling. "You are always the gentleman. I love you for that."

"And I love you, my sweet," he murmured, pressing a kiss to her hand.

He poured the wine into the only two glasses Wren owned, broke the bread, and then served her cheese from the edge of a knife Jemmy had given her. They ate by the light of a single taper, and it was magical. Wren had rarely known such peace.

Much later, as the candle flame burned low, Wren and Laney enjoyed long moments of just being together.

"I think I have been blessed," she whispered.

Laney smiled. "I know I have been." He reached out,

threading one hand through her hair. He massaged her neck, love in his gaze.

Suddenly, though, his movements stilled when he felt the clasp of the chain and pendant she now wore.

"What is this?" he asked innocently.

Wren stiffened. *Why, oh why hadn't she tucked away the pendant with the notes?*

Laney, unaware of her careening thoughts, lifted the chain, and then gazed down at the pendant dangling from it.

"My God," he breathed at sight of it.

Wren, fearing he would know she'd stolen the thing, held her breath.

But the look on his face was not one of censure but rather pain . . . and disbelief.

"What is it, Laney?" she asked, leaning forward, worry creasing her brow. "You look as though you've seen a ghost."

Laney shook his head, rifling one hand through his burnished hair. "I fear I have at that," he breathed. "My God," he said again. "I suddenly remember."

"Remember *what?*" Wren asked.

"My past," he said. "Or at least a part of it."

Wren immediately reached up to unclasp the pendant, and then she spilled the chain and the silver sphere into Laney's opened palm. "Tell me," she urged. "What do you remember?"

"I—I am not exactly certain. A feeling, I guess. Of trust and love."

"What else, Laney?"

"That's it, that's all. Damme, but that pendant reminds me of something . . . of someone. I—I can't explain it!"

"Then don't try to do so," Wren whispered, soothing

him. "Your memory will return, in time. I have no doubt about that."

"But when?" he muttered, suddenly sounding as though he'd been tortured with fleeting memories for too long.

Wren knew then that even though she might be free of Madame Blue, her life wouldn't be in order until Laney recovered his total memory.

The pendant was possibly a link to his past. Who had given it to Madame Blue? And why? And what did it represent in Laney's life?

She managed to convince Laney to lie down and rest. Their morning's excursion had worn him out. He was still weak from his wound. She should not have allowed him to go out, and certainly shouldn't have enticed him to chase after her. And now, the pendant had reminded him sharply of something from his past.

He'd had a long day. Dear Laney, she thought. How she loved him. She wouldn't rest until she'd uncovered his past. Even though she might lose him once he knew of his history, she was determined to help him discover who he was. She would do that for him. She would do it because she loved him more than anything . . . and because without knowing his past, they could have no future.

The wine helped lull Laney to sleep as did the fact Wren sat beside him, holding his hand. In his other fist, he still held the pendant. Clutched it, actually.

Wren wondered how Madame Blue had come to own the pendant. Wondered, too, what link it proved to Laney's past.

What irony that the very thing Wren had stolen from the strongbox was also the reason she could not now return to Madame Blue's. If the older woman ever learned of Wren's thievery, she would doubtless summon the authorities and see to it Wren was thrown into prison.

Wren frowned, wishing she could return to the brothel and demand to know how the madame had acquired the pendant. But to do such a thing would be to take a dangerous route and place herself in more peril.

Perhaps come morning and after a night of sleep, Laney would remember more about his past. For the moment, it was Wren's only hope.

Feeling bone-weary, Wren rose to her feet, stretched, and then reached for the pitcher near the bed. She decided to go downstairs and fetch some fresh water, feeling the need to clean the scent of Madame Blue's house from her skin.

The hallway had darkened considerably since the time she and Laney had returned home. Wren shivered, feeling a coolness she hadn't felt while inside her room. She thought about going back inside for her cloak, knowing the air would be cooler once she was outside near the water pump, but she was too tired to bother.

She headed down the narrow flight of stairs.

A man loitered along the landing, leaning against the wall.

He was large, dark-haired, and looked menacing.

Wren's heart seemed to stop beating as she immediately came to a pause on the steps. She felt paralyzed with fear.

"Dear God," she breathed, recognizing the man as one of Madame Blue's henchman.

The ugly man grinned.

Before Wren could turn and run, even before she could cry out for Laney, the man heaved himself away from the wall and lunged toward her. He caught her in a startling, strong hold, twisted her about and then pressed the tip of a knife against her ribcage. The pitcher fell, its handle breaking as it met with the hard wood of the landing.

"If you call out or fight, you'll die," the man warned, even as he started down the stairs, dragging her with him.

Before she knew it, Wren was forced outside to the street where one of Madame Blue's enclosed carriages awaited them. She was thrust inside as the door was slammed shut behind her. Inside she was met with another devilish-eyed man. He forced a cloth bag over her head, held it fast and tight, and then waited for Wren to suffer the horrid, dizzying effects of little oxygen.

A whip cracked outside the carriage, and then suddenly they were moving swiftly down the street, away from Laney and the boardinghouse, and heading fast for a destination Wren could only surmise was Madame Blue's house of ill repute.

Thirteen

Larkin spent the morning seeing to the details of a marriage . . . a marriage that would unite him with Meredith. He could hardly believe he was actually going to go through with the idea. 'Twas insanity on his part, surely.

But he continued with his morning's work, purchasing a special license and then finding a rector willing to perform a marriage service on such short notice.

By midday, everything was set. They could be married on the morrow, if that was Meredith's wish, which it would be, Larkin knew. She was very anxious to wed Laney. Indeed, Miss Meredith Darlington was very much in love with the third Earl of Graystone.

This last thought brought a prick of pain deep in his soul, but Larkin forced it away. He had no claim to Meredith or her affections—even if he wished otherwise.

He returned home for the noon meal, not much in the mood for the company of others, and was met there with an urgent missive. The note was from Mr. Michael Selwyn, the solicitor whom he'd not only entrusted with the duty of being a liaison between himself and the hired investigators looking for Laney, but also with the secret of his actual identity. Selwyn had proved to be a man Larkin could trust.

Though Selwyn's note did not go into detail, it was

very clear to Larkin there had obviously been some headway made in the search for his brother. In fact, there seemed the greatest possibility Laney had been found.

Larkin directed a footman to see to it that his horse was at the door in ten minutes. He immediately headed for Holywell Street, a barrage of conflicting emotions pumping through him.

Laney, found. Dear God, let it be so! he prayed.

But on the heels of this came the sobering realization that once Laney returned, Larkin would no longer have any reason to be a part of Meredith's life.

Too, she would have to be told the truth about Larkin's duplicity.

Meredith would doubtless hate him for taking on the identity of his brother, Larkin knew. She would feel deceived. Perhaps she would even feel shame remembering the kiss they'd shared in Lady Darcy's garden—a kiss she had responded to with quick passion.

Yes, there would be the devil to pay once Laney was safely home and the truth was told to both he and Meredith. Larkin would have much to explain, and he guessed that neither Laney or Meredith would react happily to the news of Larkin wooing his brother's chosen lady.

Their initial reactions would not be the worst of it, though. The worst would come later and would last a lifetime . . . the worst would be facing a life without Meredith in it.

It was with these rioting thoughts in his head that Larkin made haste to Holywell Street.

Meredith was surprised when Lord Thornwood paid a call shortly before noon. Stubbins delivered the man's card to her upon a silver salver, fully expecting Meredith to turn the man away as she was in a hurry to be off to Lady Darcy's for a very important nuncheon.

"Shall I tell his lordship you are not receiving?" asked the man.

Meredith shook her head. "No, that won't be necessary. I shall speak with him, but only briefly," Meredith replied, thinking that perhaps his lordship might have come to talk more about Julianne. She headed for the front sitting room.

Lord Thornwood, garbed in a superbly cut charcoal coat, tight-fitting, white kerseymere breeches, and with a gleaming gold pin nestled in his perfect neckcloth, bowed at the sight of her. "Thank you for seeing me, Miss Darlington," he said.

"You are most welcome, my lord, but I must admit you've caught me at a busy moment. I was just about to take my leave."

"Oh?"

Meredith had the distinct impression he was very much interested in where—and with whom—she might be spending her afternoon. "Yes. I . . . I have a previous engagement," she responded.

"Ah," he murmured. "Doubtless it is with Lord Graystone."

Meredith lifted one brow, surprised by the mans audacity in even asking.

"Lord Graystone," Meredith answered, her own impervious tone surprising her,—"has, I'm told, business to discuss with his solicitor on Holywell Street this day. As for myself, I have been invited to share the noon meal with a few close friends."

His lordship obviously noted Meredith's sudden coolness just as he obviously sought to soothe over the moment with yet another apology for his unplanned visit. He then turned the topic of conversation to Miss Beveridge, and inquired if the same was still intending to visit the balloon ascension.

Meredith assured him that Julianne's plans had not changed as far as she knew. They then chatted of nothing in particular, mostly of the card-party and the fact he claimed to be very pleased he'd made her acquaintance and had had the pleasure of playing whist with Miss Beveridge and herself.

And then, just as unexpectedly as he'd arrived, he took his leave.

Meredith still had not puzzled out his visit when she ordered for the carriage to be brought round. There was something about Lord Thornwood's presence today that unsettled her and left a lingering of doubt about him. Perhaps he wasn't the best choice for the gentle-hearted Julianne. But no, Meredith thought, she was surely being ridiculous. His lordship had done nothing to invite her suspicion . . . and yet, remembering Laney's reaction to the man's presence at Lady Darcy's caused Meredith a moment of indecision.

Meredith shook away the feeling. She was just in high fidgets due to her meeting with the Midnight Society and their latest endeavor, she told herself. That was all. Nothing more.

Later, Meredith, Peach, and Lady Darcy lingered over the nuncheon at Lady Darcy's townhouse, none of them much in the mind of eating. They'd gathered together nearly two hours prior to discuss plans for the Midnight

Society. However, their latest plan had not met with success and now the three of them were not in the best of spirits.

"It would seem we're at an impasse," said Lady Darcy. "How can we aid this woman named Suzanne if she won't even speak with Stubbins?"

"He believes she has an aversion to anyone of the male gender," explained Peach, "and I cannot particularly fault the girl for that considering what she's had to endure in her young life, and all at the hands of men with few if any morals." Peach let out a sigh. "It pains me to think of what will become of her and her little boy."

Meredith, who had been silent for several moments, finally spoke up. "We cannot just stop now," she said. "Surely there must be something more we can do!"

"I don't know what," said Lady Darcy. "Your Stubbins has gone so many times to that part of Town he'll soon be a common fixture there. Besides, the girl hasn't accepted our offers as of yet, what makes us believe she will do so anytime soon? The female doesn't seem to truly want our aid at this time, Meredith. Perhaps in the future she will, but for now she does not. I make a motion we move on and find someone who feels a more pressing need to be free of the ties that bind them. We cannot, after all, force anyone to accept our aid. That is not the purpose of the Midnight Society. We created our group in order to offer aid to fellow women who want to take part in it. We did not create this society to change anyone's beliefs or even to make them want other things. We are here to help those who wish to empower themselves and know a better life."

"Lady Darcy is right," Peach added softly to Meredith.

"My dear Merry, I know you are deeply concerned about this woman and her young son, but we must face the fact that now and again our missions won't be successful. This, I am afraid, is one of those times. We must forget about Suzanne and her boy, and think of others whom we can aid. And there *will* be others, Meredith."

Meredith nodded, though she wasn't in total agreement with her friends. She'd talked with Stubbins and had heard with her own ears the tale of the woman named Suzanne. Stubbins said the young woman had been terribly frightened and clearly not wanted to continue her work at the house of ill repute known as Madame Blue's. He said she'd been particularly concerned about her son and his future. Stubbins was of the mind that Suzanne was on the verge of accepting the aid of the Midnight Society but he felt she would most likely only accept if a woman were to visit with her and make the offer of help.

Meredith, knowing that neither Peach nor Lady Darcy would approve of any members of the Midnight Society traveling out to speak with Suzanne, decided not to even suggest such a thing.

Instead, she decided she would just do so on her own.

A half-hour later, Meredith was in her carriage, heading for Holywell Street and creating a plan of sorts. She knew, from Stubbins's account, that Suzanne was always in the kitchens of Madame Blue's precisely at 9 P.M. every evening for that is when she sneaked away from the guests to share a cup of chocolate with her son before tucking him into bed. If Meredith arrived at that appointed hour, she could simply approach the kitchen entrance, find Suzanne and none would be the wiser. She might even be able to retrieve the woman and her boy that very night without being discovered by any of Madame Blue's employees.

Then again, she might not.

Who knew what despicable people lurked around such a place in the evening. That, of course, was the reason Meredith decided she wouldn't be sending her maid in her stead. There was no possible way she would risk Betsy to such a lawless part of London. As for herself, she was fairly confident she could see to her own welfare, and if she had Boyle drive her in an enclosed carriage then perhaps all would go as hoped. Boyle would certainly keep a safe eye on her.

But there was, Meredith knew, another person she must consider; now that Laney had said they would marry, she was not only putting her own reputation at risk with her plot of helping Suzanne, but she was also risking Laney's reputation. The future wife of the third Earl of Graystone should not be stealing about near the docks, alone and unchaperoned.

Perhaps she should tell Laney the truth. Once they were married he would eventually have to be told about her involvement with the Midnight Society. After all, the point of her marrying was so that she could claim her entire inheritance and truly do some good for the many women and children the Midnight Society was devoted to aiding.

That *was* the point of marrying Laney, wasn't it? she demanded of herself.

Of a sudden, Meredith wasn't so certain.

Now that she'd met Laney again, she found he had the ability to affect her far more deeply, and on a purely

emotional level, than she'd ever expected or even anticipated. The feelings he evoked in her were new and
strange . . . even wondrous. And they were frightening,
too.

Was this, perhaps, how it felt to truly fall in love? she
wondered.

The closer her carriage came to Holywell Street, the
more confused Meredith's thoughts became. A few days
ago, the idea of a marriage betwixt Laney and herself
had seemed sweetly simple; a perfect solution to her di-
lemma. But when he'd kissed her, and she had instinctively responded to the warmth and softness of his lips,
a marriage between them no longer seemed so simple.
From the moment their mouths had melded together,
Meredith knew there suddenly existed between them
something more than just their friendship of the past.
She could no longer think of him as the "dear, sweet
Laney" of her youth. Instead, he'd become far more. He
was a man with yearnings, a man with a powerful mag-
netism . . . and she, God help her, was physically drawn
to him, to his lips, to his touch. He made her ache to
fully experience the total scope of being a woman.

Feeling antsy and needing to do something other than
sit, Meredith instructed Boyle to pull to one side of the
street. "I think I shall walk the rest of the way," she said
to Boyle as he helped her disembark. "Take a short drive
and then return for me, won't you?"

Boyle hesitated. "Are you certain, Miss Meredith? I
shouldn't leave you alone."

"I'll be fine," Meredith insisted. "The street is filled
with people bustling about. I shall be perfectly safe."

Boyle reluctantly did as he was instructed. Meredith
watched as the carriage moved on ahead of her. With a

shake of her head and a twirl of her parasol, she moved on down the street, wondering what Boyle's reaction would be when she told him of her plan to enter a house of ill repute—and that *he* would be driving her there.

She wondered, too, what Laney might do if he learned of her planned mission. She still hadn't decided whether or not to tell him what she intended this night.

"Ah, well," she said aloud to herself, trying to buoy her spirits, and ease her conscience, "I still have the space of a few more buildings before I have to make *that* decision."

She did decide, however, not to walk too fast.

Larkin sat across from Mr. Michael Selwyn, quietly listening to the man speak.

"It appears," said Selwyn, "that his lordship is very much alive. He was seen near the docks this morning. Your man followed him, but . . ." Selwyn shook his brown-haired head, clearly struggling with how to explain the situation.

"But what, exactly?" Larkin asked, his voice low. The minute he'd heard Laney was alive, he'd been besieged with hope, yet the look on Selwyn's face was less than comforting and Larkin suddenly feared what news would come next.

"Out with it, man! Just say it and be done with it. Has my brother come to further harm?" Larkin demanded.

"No, sir, that's not it at all. At least, I don't believe so." Selwyn frowned. "The fact of the matter is, sir, the investigator lost sight of them shortly after he'd spied your brother. They, uh, managed to elude him."

"They? My brother was not alone?"

"He was in the company of a woman. Your man has yet to learn anything more about her than what he saw. She was blonde of hair, pretty, but her clothes were unremarkable and not of high fashion. He did say she seemed to be familiar with that area of Town. He also said she was aware they were being followed, and it was she who led his lordship into a building where she managed to lose the two of them in the crowded place. By the time your man pushed his own way through the throng, your brother and the female were gone. I just received this news, and was told he will continue to search for his lordship. Unfortunately, though, he hasn't many clues to follow. He did say, though, that your brother didn't appear to be held captive in any way, sir, other than . . . uh . . . being captivated by the woman."

Larkin said nothing for a full minute, only made a steeple of his fingers beneath his chin and stared hard at Selwyn, not actually seeing him.

"This makes no sense," he finally said. "None at all. Why would my brother willingly remain near the docks? If he is able, why does he not simply return home?"

Selwyn, of course, had no answers and in truth Larkin did not expect any from the man.

Larkin raked one hand through his coppery hair, expelling a long breath of hair. "Devil take it," he said, "I should not have left the task of finding my brother to anyone other than myself."

But even as he said the words, Larkin knew he'd done what he'd thought best at the time. He had come to London in his brother's guise in hopes of ferreting out the person who'd tried to see both he and Laney dead. But thus far all he'd managed to do was fall in love with

Meredith, and he certainly wasn't any closer to proving whether or not Lord Thornwood was the culprit who'd hired some lawless thugs to ambush himself and Laney.

Well, he would right all of that today, Larkin determined, getting to his feet.

"Sir?" said Selwyn, rising as well. "What do you intend?"

Larkin's green eyes burned with a dark fire. "To find my twin—with or without the help of any investigators. Obviously my brother has come out of hiding. There must be *someone* who also spied him and knows something concerning his whereabouts."

"One would think so," agreed Selwyn, rather nervously. "However, I must say the investigators you hired are the best at their business, irregardless of what you must be thinking now. They've never failed in their pursuits. It is my opinion—if I may be so bold to say so, sir—that his lordship either does not wish to be found or else hasn't a clue of who he is and where he truly belongs. To be shot and left for dead must certainly be a horrid thing, sir. One could come to the conclusion that his lordship's nearly fatal wound has perhaps muddled his thinking."

Larkin frowned; he'd begun to suspect the very possibility Selwyn was proposing.

"You are quite right, my good man," he finally replied. "I cannot imagine what other reason my brother would have for not returning home. But whatever the deuce it is, I intend to find him this day. If I must knock on every door in every building along the docks, I shall do so. Indeed, I fear I should have done exactly that the night he was shot."

"I pray you will not torture yourself over what you

'should have done,' sir," said Selwyn. "You have competently managed his lordship's affairs these past many weeks. In fact, begging my pardon for saying so, you have created profits for his lordship he might not have realized if not for your sharp thinking. When his lordship returns home, he will find his estates have been keenly managed."

That said, Selwyn quickly scrawled the address of the place where Laney had last been seen, then handed the paper to Larkin.

"I wish you well, sir, and I'll certainly keep you informed of any further details I might hear concerning your brother," said Selwyn.

Larkin thanked the man and then headed outside.

He was surprised to see Meredith strolling down the street toward him.

B'god, but she appeared a vision with her white parasol reflecting the sunlight and creating a blazing halo about her head. She wore a gown of green-spotted white muslin, a small spencer that fit her to perfection, and a wide-brimmed bonnet that served to call attention to her beauteous features and riot of blond curls. She did not, however, wear her spectacles and so did not immediately recognize him.

Pity, he thought, as he rather liked the look of her with her spectacles slipping down the bridge of her prettily shaped nose. He would again like the opportunity to reposition those spectacles; in fact, he would like any reason at all to draw physically nearer to her.

Larkin waited until Meredith was nearly abreast of him before he said her name. Whispered it, in fact. He touched one hand to the brim of his tall top hat as she stopped, her parasol slanted back atop one shoulder, a sudden smile on her lips.

"Good day, my lord," she said, sounding pleased by the sight of him, yet looking rather surprised to see him as a few passersby hurried on about their business. The two of them might be having a chance meeting, rather than the rendezvous they'd planned.

"Greetings, Miss Darlington," he replied formally, yet he could feel the warmth filling his own eyes as he gazed at her. His blood surged at her nearness.

The two of them began a leisurely pace, and for all the world it appeared they were merely headed in the same direction and had only just decided to stroll a block or two in each other's company.

"I am exceedingly glad to see you," he murmured, smiling. He truly meant the words. For the first time since he'd taken on Laney's role, he'd said something that was in his own heart and not what he thought proper for Laney to say.

"And I you," she replied, just as softly.

Larkin's heart did an odd flip-flop at her words. Gad, how he hated she thought he was another. How he despised having to woo her in his brother's guise. But it was Laney, and not he, whom she wished to marry, to share a life. Larkin knew a moment of deep and unfathomable sadness.

He realized he must have been staring at her with his emotions on his sleeve, for her smile suddenly lessened in intensity.

"Is something wrong?" she asked.

He thought of Laney, thought of what would happen when his brother was found, and he knew a disheartening melancholy. Meredith would despise him once the truth was known, and with good reason.

He tried to shake off his sadness. "It is nothing," he told her. The words felt exactly as the lie they were.

He and Meredith approached an intersection of a side road. Larkin offered her his arm, intending to help her across the lanes of traffic. She placed her gloved hand in the crook of his arm, and the feel of it there was as right as the sun on them and the light breeze ruffling past.

"I have spent the morning procuring a special license and making the arrangements for us to be married," he said.

"Dear Laney," she breathed, clearly happy, though her fingers trembled atop his sleeve, "how like you to immediately see to things."

"Unfortunately, though," he went on, "it won't be St. George's or any other fashionable place of worship where we recite our vows. 'Tis a small church whose rector is willing to perform the service at such short notice."

"It will be perfect," she insisted, her words sounding breathless and shyly pleased.

The tightness in Larkin's breast grew in intensity. "I shall make the ceremony as pleasing as possible. Indeed, I have spent the latter half of the morning seeing to every detail. I thought the small church should be filled with flowers. It is only right," he finished, thinking of their stolen kiss in Lady Darcy's town house gardens.

"Yes," she murmured. "Lots and lots of flowers. After all, the two of us first met, alone, on a night filled with the scent of the earth's flowers. And did we not tell one and all we'd spent that night enjoying the written word in your father's garden?"

Larkin, not at all a part of the memories she had of Laney and what they'd shared, felt tortured. He wanted this marriage ceremony to be something that reminded Meredith of what the two of them had shared, not Laney. And yet . . it was Laney, not himself, whom she was so willing to marry.

And it was Laney for whom he had come to London in the first place, he forcefully reminded himself. Meredith was of the mind Laney would marry her in the name of friendship—and for all Larkin knew, Laney would have done just that.

As they stepped off the curb and onto the street, Larkin felt as though he was stepping off the edge of the world. There was so much he wished to say to this woman. So much he wanted her to know. *He* desired to be the one to marry her and hold her heart forever. *He* wanted to share a marriage bed with her.

As they headed across the lane, Larkin said suddenly, "Before we marry, Meredith, there is something I must tell you. I—I have racked my brain about this, yet I know I cannot stand before all that is holy without telling you the truth. You see, there is something I must do this day, something that has been left undone but when finished will affect you—and me—greatly."

Meredith surprised him by coming to a standstill in the lane, her amber eyes—eyes that could not lie—suddenly filling with a purpose. "Dear Laney," she replied, "there is something *I,* too, must tell you, something that will also affect us and our lives together."

Larkin could not imagine what that something could be, but he hoped and prayed the truth would be that she'd come to love him not for the memories she and Laney had shared, but because she loved the man he now was.

"Tell me," he uttered. "Tell me what is on your mind and in your heart, Meredith."

She took a deep breath, clearly gathering courage. She never had a chance to say the words however, for just then she spied something behind him and she opened her mouth in horror.

Larkin immediately twisted his head about. He saw a lathered team of horses and a carriage out of control careening down upon them. He thought he heard Meredith cry out his brother's name, but he couldn't be certain for suddenly his mind was filled with the clatter of onrushing wheels, the whinny of horses, and the horrid sound of a driver yelling for all to step clear.

Larkin immediately grabbed for Meredith. He spun her lithe body about, pushing her forward, out of the line of danger. The two of them crashed to the ground just as the runaway carriage charged past, missing them by mere inches.

Meredith's parasol, knocked free of her hold in the fall, was sucked under the carriage wheels. Its handle splintered into two halves, the pristine fabric torn apart and sullied by hooves and wheels and the dirt of the street.

Meredith hit the ground with a muffled cry of pain. Larkin had tried to cushion her but had failed. "Are you all right, Meredith?"

She looked dazed and stunned and too precious for words. "I—I think so."

Larkin immediately got to his feet, not caring about his own possible injuries. He saw that one sleeve of her gown had been ripped where her elbow had scraped the pavement. A bright spot of crimson blood showed from where her skin had been lightly torn by the impact.

Larkin yanked off his necktie, then kneeled beside her, pressing the too-starched linen to her elbow. "Dear God. You've been cut."

"Only scraped, I assure you."

"You could have been killed!"

She managed a weak, tremulous smile, and again assured him she was fine. By now, several gentlemen had come rushing to their aid and even a young lad hawking the news ran toward them, asking if he should run for help.

Meredith assured everyone she was fine. Her eyes met Larkin's. "Truly, I am not seriously injured, only shaken," she whispered.

Larkin wasn't mollified. "I'll hunt down that driver," he declared in a passion. "I'll make certain he pays for his recklessness!"

"My lord," she gasped, appalled by his vow. "Please. It was clearly an accident. The man's team must have been spooked. 'Twas a freak accident, nothing more."

Larkin did not agree. This was no mere accident! Someone had tried to kill him once, and his brother as well. Clearly, that same someone was not willing to leave the deeds undone.

As he helped Meredith to her feet, Larkin felt the precious pendant he wore—now hanging upon a new chain—slap against his chest. The feel of it reminded him of the cutthroats whom he and Drake met upon the docks that night in July, and remembered too the man named Bart had wanted Larkin's pendant as proof of having succeeded in murdering him.

There were only a handful of people who knew about the silver spheres Laney and Larkin had been given by

Amabel on the day of their births; three of those people were now dead. One remained.

"Thornwood." The name came past Larkin's lips with a hiss.

"What?" Meredith asked, confused by his sudden outburst.

"Nothing," Larkin answered, remembering himself. He gazed hard at her. "Are you certain you are fine?"

She nodded just as her carriage and its driver turned down the lane where they stood. Larkin dabbed at her scrapes with the cloth, then resolutely led her to the door of her landau. Even if he'd brought his own carriage to Holywell Street, he would not have dared take Meredith home himself for he feared he'd placed her in harm's way by even being near her. He would not risk doing so again.

Meredith was clearly reluctant to leave his side. She waited until the strangers who'd come to help had dispersed, then she spoke.

"Laney," she whispered. "I'm perfectly all right. I don't wish to part company with you just yet. There is so much we have to talk about and plan this day. I hate to leave you like this. Please, know that I am fine and—"

"Not another word," he said. "I would rather you go home now. I would rather you were safe within the walls of your own rooms."

"You—you are frightening me, Laney," she said even as he helped her up into her carriage. "Surely what happened was an accident."

"Go home, Meredith. Stay there. And do not, I pray you, leave your safe haven—not for anyone."

Her amber eyes narrowed. "You fear someone," she stated. "You uttered Lord Thornwood's name. You think he might have had something to do with this foul accident, don't you?"

He couldn't lie to her, but he couldn't tell her the truth either . . . for the truth was something which was not entirely certain.

"Go," he repeated. "Stay at home and await word from me."

"I shall go," she said finally and with great reluctance. "But you must promise to come to me soon, and with an explanation.

"I will," Larkin said, stepping back and giving her coachman the nod to be gone.

Larkin watched as Meredith's carriage took off at a fast pace. He blew out a breath, closing his eyes, knowing he couldn't tell Meredith the truth until his brother was found and the culprit apprehended.

Such a scenario could take an hour . . . or a lifetime.

Until then, he had the added task of protecting Meredith. He'd made the foolish mistake of ensnaring the marriageable Miss Meredith in his coil. Clearly, his enemy now knew that wherever Meredith might be, Larkin was sure to follow.

Larkin was almost certain Lord Thornwood was the villain, and it bode ill that the man had shown interest in Meredith. Larkin must take measures to ensure she would not be alone with Thornwood, or even in his company for that matter.

He knew of only one person whom he could trust to oversee Meredith's safety and do so without Meredith even knowing she was being guarded: Sir Harry Drake.

He found Drake at the club, explained the happenings of the day and his decision to scour the docks once again for his brother.

"I can't say how long I'll be gone, but I do know I shan't return without my brother," Larkin said. "I can, in my absence, trust Miss Darlington's welfare to you, Drake?"

"You can at that," his friend assured him. "Shouldn't be such a difficult task since you requested her to remain at home until she hears word from you. It is not as if she is about to go gadding off alone, into the depths of night, eh?"

Larkin had to agree. Within moments, he was riding fast for the docks.

Fourteen

Meredith grew more restless as the afternoon edged into evening and she heard no word from Laney. She worried for his safety, wondering if perhaps she'd been correct in assuming he thought their near-brush with death to have been no accident but rather a plot against him.

Surely her imagination was getting the best of her, though. Why would Lord Thornwood, of all people, wish to harm Laney? It made no sense. Meredith decided she was just in high fidgets. She was nervous, that was all. And feeling guilty.

Very guilty.

She should have told Laney about her decision to travel to a brothel and retrieve a courtesan and her son. Good Lord! Even thinking about what she intended seemed preposterous. Little wonder she hadn't told Laney. He'd have thought her as addlepated as she now felt.

By eight o'clock she knew Laney would not be appearing on her doorstep with any explanations. Meredith felt a bit miffed he hadn't sent word, or even come calling, as she had asked him to do. Well, she could not simply wile away the night waiting for him. She had a mission to attend . . . one she was determined to see through to its end.

She ordered Boyle to bring round the enclosed carriage. The man was not pleased with his mistress's request, but ever the faithful servant and knowing how determined she could be when her mind was set, he did as instructed and promised to safeguard her. Meredith trusted Boyle completely.

All will be fine, she kept saying to herself as they set off into a darkening night. Though she was feeling bruised and battered from the incident on Holywell Street, she felt a surge of excitement sweep over her as they drew nearer to the river area. Unquestionably, Meredith enjoyed her involvement with the Midnight Society, and it made her heart swell as she thought of the good she could bring to the lives of Suzanne and her son.

But of course, she remembered, Suzanne must first be willing to accept the offer of aid. . . .

As they left the heart of town, Meredith caught sight of a carriage following them. Whom could it be? Meredith gave Boyle instructions to weave in and around the next few alleys, and soon they managed to elude whoever was following them.

Meredith's nerves began to wind tighter.

Boyle eased the carriage to a halt in the lane behind the brothel at precisely five minutes before nine. He got down off his bench, hurrying to help Meredith alight.

She saw the beads of perspiration glistening upon his brow and knew a moment of unease. "I shall be perfectly fine," she assured her coachman. "No harm will come to me. Suzanne is always in the kitchens at this time of night and her coworkers are . . . uh . . . most likely preoccupied abovestairs. I doubt I shall encounter anyone other than the woman and her son, Boyle, so please, try not to worry."

"I'll cease worrying when I see you safely back home, Miss Meredith," he said.

She tried to ease his mind with a smile. "Think of this as a lark, Boyle. A story to tell someday."

"I'll not be telling this to anyone!" he assured her, his voice shaded with just a hint of censure.

Meredith decided there was no soothing him, and so, donning a black lace mask, she turned and hurried into the night. She found the back gate to be unlocked, then picked her way through the darkness to the brightly lit building. She wished she'd thought to bring her spectacles for she had a deuce of a time trying not to trip over the uneven walkway. Soon enough, though, she was at the back entrance. She dared to peek inside one nearby window and was relieved to see a stunningly dressed young woman sharing a cup of chocolate with a small, smiling boy.

Suzanne.

Meredith reached for the latch of the door. Once again, her entry was not barred. She said a quick prayer of thanks, and then pushed the portal open and stepped inside.

The woman swung around, her eyes wide.

Meredith held one finger to her lips. She removed her mask as she quietly shut the door behind her. "Hello, Suzanne. My name is Meredith Darlington. Please, do not be alarmed. I've come to help you and your son. I am a member of the Midnight Society."

At this last bit of information, Suzanne visibly relaxed. She turned to the boy, saying, "Willy, sweetheart, be a good boy and go to your room. Gather up your special blanket and then wait for me, will you? I'll come tuck you into bed in a few moments."

The boy, staring curiously at Meredith, slid off his chair and then did as he was asked.

Meredith waited until he was out of the room before speaking again. To Suzanne, she said, "I've a carriage waiting outside, one that will take you far and fast away from this place if that is your wish. We've a safehouse in the country, a few hours from Town, where you and Willy can live for as long as is necessary. You'll want for nothing. There is plenty of food and clothing, and there is schooling for the many children there, and for you, too, if you'd like. We want to help you, Suzanne. We want to offer you a new start in life. Please, won't you come with me now?"

The young woman was suddenly crying. "Oh, dear God, yes," she breathed. *"Yes.* A—another person had sought to help me this day by seeing I had money enough to leave, but I—I grew scared and later replaced the money. Since then I've been regretting my decision! Now I am doubly glad you've come!" Suzanne's tears increased as she thanked Meredith over and over for coming to her aid.

Meredith felt her own eyes become wet with tears. How wonderful it felt to be able to help others. She moved forward, taking Suzanne's shaking hands in hers. "Can you be ready to go in a few minutes? I don't know where your room is, but I don't think you should risk going abovestairs."

"No . . . no, I shouldn't," said Suzanne, trembling still. "I—I don't care about my own things. I don't have much, anyway. But Willy. He has a few toys that are dear to him. And his blanket. We cannot leave without his special blanket."

"And so we shan't," Meredith assured her.

Suzanne looked at her with wide, tortured eyes. "But what about my—my employer? Madame Blue will be furious. I—I am afraid of what she'll try and do once she learns of my flight."

Meredith squeezed Suzanne's hands. "There will be *nothing* she can do, do you hear? Nothing at all. This place I shall take you to is tucked away in the country. It is a very secretive place. Once there, you will learn skills of some sort, and the members of my group will see to it you find employment somewhere other than London. Your former employer will not be able to locate you, that I promise. And you and Willy will know a new life."

"But I am so afraid," Suzanne said. "I don't want to lose my son . . ."

"You *won't* lose him," Meredith assured her. "I shall personally see to that. I shall do everything in my power to ensure that you and Willy remain together . . . and are safe."

"Why?" Suzanne whispered. "Why would you do such a thing for someone you don't even know?"

Suddenly, the inner door of the kitchen was thrust open and a woman with golden blond hair and wearing a gown of crimson velvet, entered. She was followed by two brutish-looking fellows. "Why indeed?" the woman demanded.

Suzanne shrank back, terrified. "Madame Blue!"

The woman smiled thinly. "Surprised to see me, my lovely Suzanne? You shouldn't be. I have, in a room upstairs, a fellow conspirator of yours." Her smile smeared into a sneer. "I know you were with Wren when she robbed me this day. She stole something very dear, in fact. You shall pay for your part in her thievery, and also for the fact you thought to leave here now without ever telling me."

Meredith, unwilling to cower in the face of the painted, frightening woman and her henchman, stepped in front of Suzanne. "Whatever is your intent, do forget it," she warned, her own bravado amazing her. "Suzanne is not your property. You cannot dictate her life."

"Oh? I beg to differ. Whoever you are, you aren't soon to be leaving." The woman gave a nod of her head to the men standing near. They moved forward, each of them roughly taking hold of Meredith and Suzanne.

"Now see here!" Meredith exploded. "You have no right to treat us in such a way. You—"

"On the contrary," Madame Blue savagely cut in, "I have every right. You see, Suzanne is a favored pet of my many customers." Her gaze raked the tearful Suzanne. "You didn't actually believe I'd let you go, did you, my dear? As for what you watched Wren do this day in my office, I have not yet decided what penance you'll be forced to pay. As a matter of fact, that you'd planned to flee here with this woman as your guide bothers me more than Wren's petty thievery!"

"I—I am sorry," Suzanne said.

"Sorry?" Madame Blue thundered. "Sorry 'tis not enough, not by far!"

Suzanne quivered, crying all the more.

Meredith, struggling to be free of the brute's hold on her, glared at the woman. "How dare you frighten and belittle Suzanne like this! I demand that you let us go. I—"

"Shut your mouth," Madame Blue spat. To her men, she ordered, "Take them upstairs. Keep them quiet. And get the boy as well." She glared at Meredith, adding to her men, "Afterall, I wouldn't want a child and his mother to be parted."

Suzanne gave a moan of despair, fearing for her son's life.

Meredith was forced out of the kitchen and roughly pushed up several flights of back stairs to Madame Blue's own private wing where she was unceremoniously shoved into an elegant and low-lit chamber. Suzanne and a frightened Willy soon followed. The door was slammed against them, and a key could be heard turning sharply in the lock.

"Mama?" Willy called.

"I am here," Suzanne whispered, gathering her son in a tight hug. "I'm here, Willy."

Meredith sucked in a gasp of air. Sweet Lord, what had she led this woman and her child into? She must get them free.

Meredith spied the window, and the sheets atop the bed, and wondered if she dared make a rope of those sheets to toss out the window . . . and wondered, too, if Suzanne would even want to follow her now, or would dare risk having her son climb down from so high up.

Oh, God, how she wished she'd told Laney of her mission this night. How she wished he were near to lend his aid. Laney—her "new" Laney—would be able to get them out of this mess, she knew. He was ever brave and bold. He alone would know what to do.

But, alas, she'd not had a chance to tell him of her quest to aid Suzanne and Willy. Laney thought her to be home, safe in her own bed. Meredith might never see him again. There would be no chance to tell him how she'd come to love him, adore him, how she'd come to appreciate the man he'd grown to be.

Meredith knew a strong urge to cry.

Larkin had spent too many hours going from building to building alongside the docks asking questions and knocking on doors. Yet he was no closer to finding Laney than he had been when he'd left the heart of Town.

It was just a little before nine o'clock when he exited a busy tavern and headed for his horse, surprised even to find his mount untouched and his saddle intact. This part of Town was not the safest place for a man to be, and certainly was not an area where one left one's mount unattended, but luck was with him, it seemed, for there stood the horse, untouched.

Larkin swung himself up onto the saddle, guiding the beast up the street when suddenly he espied the shadow of someone fast approaching. He felt the hackles of his hair rising on the back of his neck until he saw the man's face come into the glare of the street lamps.

"*Laney?*"

"Larkin, b'god, I thought it was you!" Laney stepped near, beaming up at him.

Larkin was thunderstruck by the sight of his brother. "I learned you'd possibly been shot. I—"

"Possibly? No possibly, but most assuredly, brother of mine. Had a devil of a time recovering, too. In fact, I have spent the last months unable to remember barely a shred of my past . . until tonight, that is. Tonight, I remembered everything. I remembered *you*." Laney grinned up at him, a wild light in his eyes. "No, don't get down. Don't move. I need a fast mount at the moment."

Larkin couldn't believe his ears or his eyes. Was this truly his reserved and very proper brother standing near and wearing a sailor's shirt beneath a fine coat? And was this actually Laney who appeared so . . . so animated?

The man had Laney's looks, but few of the mannerisms Larkin remembered.

"What the deuce is going on?" Larkin demanded.

"I am in love!" Laney replied. "Amazing, is it not? But 'tis true. I am in love with a lady I must hasten to find."

Could he mean Meredith? Larkin wondered.

"Quick," Laney said, not offering Larkin any time to think. "Make room for me! I've a quest to fulfill."

Larkin, shaking his head, offered his brother a hand. Laney took it, swinging himself up and onto the saddle behind Larkin.

"Say," Laney said, "this is *my* horse, Larkin. And my saddle, to boot. And is that not my crop you're holding?"

"You are correct on all accounts," admitted Larkin.

"Care to tell me why are you sitting in my saddle, astride my horse and with my crop in your hand, Larkin?"

" 'Tis a long story, brother."

Laney gave an unexpected laugh. "Why am I not surprised?" he asked. "Gad, but the world has become a truly puzzling place since that night upon the docks when I was shot. Before then, I'd have been livid to find you wearing my threads and riding my horse. Now, though, I am just glad to see you, brother of mine!"

Larkin, though amazed at what was happening, felt his

lips turn up into a smile. He had his twin with him. All was now right in the world. He urged the horse forward.

"By the way, Laney," he managed to ask as they shot forward, "where are we headed?"

"To a brothel," Laney said, his voice suddenly serious. "To Madame Blue's to be exact. You see, my future wife is there. Turn left here, Larkin. And do hurry. I fear she's met with trouble."

Larkin did not need to be told twice.

Suddenly, the two of them were one with the wind, and it felt good, felt right. Most of all, Larkin was buoyed by the fact Laney had clearly fallen in love during his escapade alongside the docks . . and obviously the woman Laney had come to claim as his own wasn't Meredith.

Meredith, Larkin knew, would be nowhere near a brothel!

Meredith had the sheets tied together and was just depositing the long line of them out the window when the door swung open and Madame Blue, accompanied by her ugly henchmen, and another terrified but spirited female, was thrust into the room.

"I wouldn't try that, were I you," Madame Blue said in her oily voice. " 'Tis a long way down." She gave a final savage shove to the woman with her, and sent her stumbling forward.

"Wren!" Suzanne cried, rushing to catch her and break her fall.

The woman called Wren righted herself and then turned to face Madame Blue. Meredith immediately recognized Wren to be a capable adversary for the wicked courtesan.

"You won't get away with this," Wren said.

"Oh, but I will and I have," replied Madame Blue. "You robbed my strongbox and made a grave error in taking a pendant that is very dear to me."

Meredith watched as the pretty Wren stiffened. "What of that pendant, Madame Blue? What do you know of it? *To whom did it once belong?*"

"I'll let you ask the person who gave it to me," she said, stepping aside as yet another man entered the room.

He had eyes only for Wren. The glint in his gaze was decidedly dangerous. "Do you perhaps know of a certain gentleman who claims ownership of the pendant? You will tell me now where this gentleman is hiding, and you will do so quickly or else I'll be forced to lead you to one of the rooms in the other wing, where there are whips and all manner of vile things I can use to *make* you tell me."

Wren, though clearly trembling, lifted her chin, her back straightening. "No!"

The man stepped nearer. "Do not be a fool. Your life may be spared, but only if you tell me where he is. I know you are hiding a man, have been for some time."

"Who are you?" Wren demanded.

It was then Meredith stepped away from the window and out of the shadows. She was confused by Lord Thornwood's presence, and appalled at his words and behavior. "He is Lord Reginald Thornwood," Meredith said.

His lordship swung his gaze about, finally paying closer attention to the others in room. He instantly paled at sight of Meredith. "Good God," he breathed. He turned on Madame Blue. "You said nothing of *her* presence! I was only told I'd meet with the female who had too many questions about the pendant."

"You'll forgive me for not mentioning this other visitor. I haven't a clue as to who she is, but she intended to take my lovely Suzanne away, and that I will never allow to happen." said Madame Blue.

Thornwood's nostrils flared. "This woman is none other than Miss Meredith Darlington, an heiress, and a very influential one at that."

Madame Blue hesitated for only a moment, and then shrugged. "She has been a thorn in my side this night. Too, she has now seen and heard too much. She will be disposed of along with the others. We can do no less. Not now."

Meredith, panicking, looked to Lord Thornwood. "I don't know what part in this you play, but if there is any shred of decency in you, I beg of you to allow all of us to go free. The boy is frightened. He should not be witness to any of this. Let us go. Please, my lord!"

"What a pretty plea," Madame Blue cut in. "But it is not enough to save your lives. Unfortunately, the lot of you know too much. We cannot allow you to leave . . . or even to live."

She made a motion to step back, out of the room, directing Lord Thornwood to bring Wren if he wished to question her in private. She then gave her brutish fellows the go-ahead to do their dirty work with the others.

It was then three gentleman ambushed the room.

"Laney!" Meredith cried, at sight of her beloved.

But no, it wasn't just Laney, but rather *two* of him, and a third man who was older but solidly built and capable of swinging a punch.

The next moments became a blur as the gentlemen

made quick work of disarming and overpowering Madame Blue's cohorts. That done, Laney—or his looka-like—pinned Lord Thornwood to a wall. The other cornered Madame Blue.

Meredith stepped toward Laney, or who she thought was Laney. *"Laney?"* she whispered, looking from him to his mirror image.

"Meredith!" he whispered, dismay and then something akin to guilt claiming his handsome features. "I don't know what the devil you're doing here, but I shall explain my presence and that of my twin as well once all of this is finished." He was holding Lord Thornwood in a death grip, and he clearly intended to vent his rage on him.

"Please," Meredith whispered, "you are frightening me by the look in your eyes, Laney."

Wren suddenly spoke. "That man is not Laney," she said to Meredith. *"This* is Laney."

Meredith turned, and she felt her knees suddenly go weak with dread as she looked into a familiar, warm face . . . a face she had fallen in love with nearly seven years prior, but one that did not now move her as the face of the man who'd pretended to be Laney.

"Hello, my merry Meredith," the true Laney said in a low voice. "It is good to see you again, though I hadn't thought to meet up with you in such a place. Life is indeed full of surprises, is it not?" He had a very un-gentlemanly hold on Madame Blue. It was clear that he, like his twin, intended to see the woman had her come-uppance.

Meredith did not move. She wondered if this was all a nightmare. "I don't understand," she said.

"I will explain," replied Laney—or rather the man

whom she'd thought to have been Laney. "I shall tell you everything, but not here and not now."

Meredith turned her gaze to him. He suddenly seemed a stranger to her.

Thornwood dared to laugh then, an ugly sound. "Can you not guess the truth, Miss Darlington?" he asked. "Take a good look at these men. They are none other than Lane and Larkin, the sons of the late second Earl of Graystone."

"Be quiet, Thornwood," Larkin warned.

"Threatening me, Larkin? Yes, I know it is you. I must say you had me fooled in believing you were Laney—just as you fooled the gentle Miss Darlington. What was it like stepping into your brother's shoes . . . wooing a woman he'd loved in the past? One must wonder what liberties you took with her, and all in Laney's name."

"B'god, Thornwood, do shut your mouth or you'll live to regret it."

"I don't think I shall live long enough to regret anything," he rasped.

"It was you who hired the villains to bring a foul end to my life and Laney's, wasn't it? And Madame Blue, she is the blond-haired messenger who saw to it a missive was delivered to me in the West Indies and another to Laney in Town."

Thornwood, sneered at him. "Yes. And it was I who hired the driver on Holywell Street."

"Bastard," Larkin breathed. "You nearly killed Miss Darlington this day."

"It is you I want dead, Larkin. I want both you and Laney out of my world. With the two of you gone," he said, "my family would no longer owe a huge debt to the Graystones. Too, I would not have to be reminded of the fact my father found your mother to be more than just a good friend. You see," he said, looking up, "Amabel and my father were very close at one time. So close, in fact, there is the very real possibility the three of us are more than just enemies . . . indeed, we are perhaps brothers of a sort."

Larkin felt his stomach churn. "Never."

Thornwood's lips thinned. "My thoughts exactly. But your mother was ever a lightskirt. She wasn't true to your father. That is why he pushed her down a flight of stairs. That is why he never reached out to her in love, but only in anger."

"Good God," Laney said, hearing now for the first time how his mother had met her end. "I had no idea. I—I had no idea of the horrid truth. Larkin, *that* is why you despised our father, why you left without so much as a word to anyone?"

Larkin nodded, his face unreadable and his gaze never leaving Thornwood's. "It is," he answered his brother. To Thornwood he said lowly, "Damn you for telling him like this, for sullying my dear mother's name. And damn you to hell for nearly running Miss Darlington down with a carriage. I should kill you for bringing harm to Meredith. Indeed, I would take great pleasure in the act."

"I wouldn't give you the satisfaction," Thornwood said, and then, in a flurry of motion, he fought to be free. He'd grabbed hold of a heavy candlestick on the table near him. He brought it up with lightning speed, slamming it against Larkin's skull.

Larkin was stunned by the blow and pushed sideways by the impact. Thornwood then raced out of the room. Larkin righted himself, intending to follow suit. There was murder in his eyes and in his mind.

"Larkin, no!" Meredith cried, reaching for him. "Do not do something you will regret. Let us just go. Let us leave this horrible place."

Larkin grabbed her by the shoulders, gently but with forceful intent, and turned her out of his path. "Stay out of this, Meredith," he said, his voice dark.

She saw the blood trickling down his face, saw the demons in his gaze. He would not stop until Thornwood was dead, she knew. "Larkin, please," she said, terrified of what he was about to do.

"Stay here," he ordered, and then he was gone, trailing after Thornwood.

Meredith rushed after them. She wasn't fast enough, though. As soon as she entered the hall, she heard a hideous howl of rage and torment. She stumbled on ahead . . . just in time to see Thornwood charge straight through a window at the end of the hallway. Glass shattered, and a horrible scream could be heard for only a second longer until suddenly, it died away. Died as Thornwood hit the ground below, the life snuffed out of him.

Meredith stopped dead in her tracks. "Sweet heaven," she whispered. "Tell me you didn't, Larkin. Tell me—"

"He jumped," Larkin said, his back to her as he stared at the curtains now blowing in the breeze through the shattered glass.

Meredith felt her shoulders sag with relief. "For a moment, I thought you might have . . ." She couldn't force herself to say the words, did not even want to consider what might have happened had Larkin murdered Lord Thornwood.

"You thought I might have killed him?" Larkin asked. "In another moment, I probably would have. You see, that is the kind of man I can be when someone threatens the lives of those I love . . . and I have come to love you, Meredith." Slowly, he turned around, facing her. "Allow me to properly introduce myself. I am the Honorable Larkin Markham Graystone, though at the moment I am feeling little honor."

Meredith was stunned. He just said he loved her. Larkin. Not Laney. She could neither move or speak. She could only stand there as wave after wave of happiness washed through her. He loved her. And she loved him.

Just then, Laney stepped into the hall. "Larkin?"

"It's over," Larkin said. "Thornwood jumped to his death. Send someone for the authorities, and tell Drake to keep a close eye on Madame Blue and her cohorts. They'll have a great deal of explaining to do once the authorities arrive. Just as I have some explanations to give."

Larkin looked at Meredith as Laney went back into the room. "Before you turn away from me in disgust, which you surely must want to do, there are some things I must say to you. I came to London in my brother's guise because someone tried to kill me and because Laney, who'd been shot, had suddenly disappeared. I thought to foul the plans of whomever that culprit might be. As it turns out, it was Thornwood; you heard his vile tale.

"I was wrong to deceive you, wrong to make you believe I was Laney. But this I vow, Meredith, from the moment I kissed you in Lady Darcy's garden, my feelings for you became totally my own. I would risk my life for my brother . . . but for you, Meredith, I would give it." He drew in a long, deep breath, a look of pain on his handsome face, and then whispered, "That is why I shall take my leave of you once I see you safely back home.

I shall not linger in Town and force you to remember what you must perceive as my ugly duplicity. I will always regret I did not meet you under different circumstances, did not have a chance of claiming your heart as my own. I only pray you will one day forgive me."

That said, he started walking back the way they'd come.

Meredith reached out, touching his sleeve, stopping him when he would have continued on. "I don't hate you, Larkin," she said softly. She lifted her gaze to his, and her eyes, she knew, were filled with the love she had for this man. She thought she heard him catch his breath as he looked into her amber eyes. "You once asked me to marry you," she said. "I answered yes, but in my heart I was thinking you weren't at all the Laney I remembered. You were something more, something new and different . . . and I told myself at that moment that I hadn't fallen in love with the Laney of my past but rather the man who was standing before me. You see, Larkin, it is you I said I would marry. Wholly and only *you.*"

Larkin placed his hand atop hers, then drew it to his lips. He kissed her palm, then her wrist, then pressed her hand against his face. "Dear God in heaven," he whispered in a prayer.

Meredith felt a wetness beneath her fingers. He was crying. "Larkin?"

"You move me to tears," he whispered, "you move me in ways no other has. *I love you, Meredith.*"

She, too, was crying.

He wrapped his arms about her, pulling her into a warm, wonderful embrace, and then he kissed her, long and lovingly, again and again and again. Meredith did not know how long they lingered in that dark, unlit hall, and she didn't care. She only knew that her world was suddenly bright and filled with promise and a love that would last a thousand lifetimes.

"I cannot wait for the two of us to marry, Larkin," she murmured.

"There is no need to wait," he said, his mouth pressing against hers even as he spoke. It seemed he could not get enough of her, or she of him. "You forget, my sweet, I purchased a special license, and on the morrow a wagon filled with flowers will be delivered to the small church I chose."

"But you bought that license in Laney's name," she reminded him.

He shook his head, pulling back to slant a smile at her. "Ah . . . no, Meredith, I didn't. I had a change of heart at the last moment and gave the man my true name. If there was going to be anyone to marry you, I decided it would be me."

She smiled, her heart light. "And what were you going to say when I saw the license?" she wondered.

Larkin kissed the tip of her nose. "To be quite honest, I hadn't a clue."

Meredith would have laughed then, but he kissed her again.

Much later, Larkin guided Meredith out of the house, along with Laney, Wren, Suzanne, and Willy. Meredith would have to tell Julianne of Thornwood's death. She frowned, thinking of what the news of the man's wickedness would do to the young woman.

"It has been a long night," Larkin said quietly to her.

"Yes," she agreed. "I was thinking of Julianne. She liked Lord Thornwood . . . or rather, she was smitten by the man he pretended to be, and she was so looking forward to the balloon ascension. We shall have to make certain she is kept busy with friends and such in the coming days."

"We will," Larkin assured her.

Drake remained inside, determined to see that Madame Blue and her men were held accountable for their attempted kidnappings, and to also explain Thornwood's death to the authorities. Drake had met up with Laney and Larkin outside the brothel earlier that night. He'd been the one trailing Meredith's carriage despite her best efforts to evade him. He'd met Boyle outside the brothel, stated his business, and the two of them had been planning a course of attack when Larkin and Laney arrived. Boyle had stayed outside in the event that Madame Blue and her cohorts tried to flee, while Laney, Larkin, and Drake hurried inside.

Boyle, now glad to see his mistress was safe, transported them all to Laney's home in Grosvenor Square. Larkin rode his own mount. Boyle then continued on to the country with Suzanne and a now-sleeping Willy. Suzanne was only too happy to be leaving the city with her son. Meredith vowed to do all she could for the two.

To the confusion of the servants, Meredith and Larkin and Laney and Wren gathered in the comfort of Laney's library. It was there Larkin fully explained his story to Laney, and Meredith explained to Larkin why she'd been at Madame Blue's.

It was then Wren's turn to tell the tale of how she and Laney had met. "I had no idea who he was," Wren finished. "In fact, I still have no idea, though I imagine he has quite a legacy considering the splendour of this home and the fact that every servant addresses him as 'my lord.' "

Larkin winked at his brother. "You've a bit of explaining to do this night yourself, I'd say."

Laney smiled. "I do at that." He reached to take hold of both Wren's hands. "I am the third Earl of Graystone, my love," he said to her. "And I am asking you to be my countess."

Wren's eyes became as wide as saucers. "A countess. *Your* countess? I believe I have just died and gone to heaven," she said, happiness in her eyes. Suddenly, though, that bright sparkle dimmed. "But my past—"

"Is now forgotten," Laney said, most sincerely. "Indeed, I found the papers you'd tucked inside the book, Wren. They shall be destroyed and no one need ever know you sang and played an instrument for the guests of that horrid house. As for the pendant you had, it is my pendant, Wren. Madame Blue must have been given the thing as payment by Thornwood when he hired a man to shoot me and leave me for dead. I remembered everything tonight as I lay upon the cot. I found your water pitcher in the stairwell and suspected foul play. It was then I hastened to Madame Blue's, fearful she'd harmed you. You see, Wren, you've made me whole and you've made me love again and to trust again. I don't care about your past. I only care about our future. You will be my countess. Say you will."

Wren's eyes misted with tears. "I want to. Desperately. But people talk, and there might be those who remember my face, remember seeing me at Madame Blue's."

"Let them talk," Laney said passionately. "I shall stare each and everyone of them down and dare them to say a word. I shall escort you about Town, introduce you to the finest families, and you shall win out. Trust me. You shall. And Meredith, she will aid us, will you not?" he asked, turning his face to her.

Meredith nodded. "I shall," she replied, understanding the love that shone in their eyes; she and Larkin shared the same. "In fact, I think my friends of the Midnight Society and at Minerva's will think you are divine."

Larkin, having been given a full account of what Meredith and her friends did at their ladies' club, feigned a groan. "Heaven help us, brother, but I fear our future wives are going to keep the two of us very busy watching over them."

"I would have it no other way," Laney insisted, smiling at Wren.

Larkin took Meredith's hand in his, their fingers threading together. "Nor would I," he said, gazing at her, his eyes darkening with passion and deep love. "No other way at all."

Meredith gave him a dazzling smile.

ZEBRA REGENCIES
ARE
THE TALK OF THE TON!

A REFORMED RAKE (4499, $3.99)
by Jeanne Savery

After governess Harriet Cole helped her young charge flee to France—and the designs of a despicable suitor, more trouble soon arrived in the person of a London rake. Sir Frederick Carrington insisted on providing safe escort back to England. Harriet deemed Carrington more dangerous than any band of brigands, but secretly relished matching wits with him. But after being taken in his arms for a tender kiss, she found herself wondering— *could* a lady find love with an irresistible rogue?

A SCANDALOUS PROPOSAL (4504, $4.99)
by Teresa DesJardien

After only two weeks into the London season, Lady Pamela Premington has already received her first offer of marriage. If only it hadn't come from the *ton's* most notorious rake, Lord Marchmont. Pamela had already set her sights on the distinguished Lieutenant Penford, who had the heroism and honor that made him the ideal match. Now she had to keep from falling under the spell of the seductive Lord so she could pursue the man more worthy of her love. Or was he?

A LADY'S CHAMPION (4535, $3.99)
by Janice Bennett

Miss Daphne, art mistress of the Selwood Academy for Young Ladies, greeted the notion of ghosts haunting the academy with skepticism. However, to avoid rumors frightening off students, she found herself turning to Mr. Adrian Carstairs, sent by her uncle to be her "protector" against the "ghosts." Although, Daphne would accept no interference in her life, she *would* accept aid in exposing any spectral spirits. What she never expected was for Adrian to expose the secret wishes of her hidden heart . . .

CHARITY'S GAMBIT (4537, $3.99)
by Marcy Stewart

Charity Abercrombie reluctantly embarks on a London season in hopes of making a suitable match. However she cannot forget the mysterious Dominic Castille—and the kiss they shared—when he fell from a tree as she strolled through the woods. Charity does not know that the dark and dashing captain harbors a dangerous secret that will ensnare them both in its web—leaving Charity to risk certain ruin and losing the man she so passionately loves . . .